Sundown

Sundown

L. R. S. Wayne

CHAPTER 1

"A evening breeze moves on high; Painting a clouldly bed of daffodils in the sky."

Gila Valley Southwest Arizona Territory 1840

A cool breeze had sprung up after the hot Arizona sun had descended down toward the blue haze-covered mountains to the Northwest, from the knoll where Ed and Ben Wiseman, each with his wife, and son on the seat beside them, had halted their wagons. The two families sat quietly for several minutes, looking down over the lush green valley unfolding below them. A crystal clear stream meandered its way through the valley, on it's way to the Gila river. Trees of various kinds covered the upper end, toward the mountains.

Finally Ed shifted in the seat, trying to give his tired rear end a rest, looked across to Ben, and said, "Well I do believe the trip was worth it. Old Jud was right when he kept saying this valley was the most beautiful place on earth, and we ought to come and claim it. Why you boys could make your fortune there. You could run thousands of cattle, and horses there." Ben took a deep breath, and shaking his head in agreement said, "I thought the flat land, and tall grass in Kansas was pretty, but this is unbelievable. Lets drive on down, make camp by that stream.

The two families had been traveling with a wagon train, on the Santa Fe trail, from St. Louis, with California as their destination. They had taken the advice of their friend, Jud Winaford, the wagon train boss, left the train in search of this wonder land he kept talking about. Delighted with their decision, they made their way down, stopping under a tall paloverde tree. After helping their wives down, the men unhitched the teams, removed the harness, led them to water. Then staked them out, to graze on the tall green grass. Ed said, "Ben if you and the boys, will gather up enough stones to build a fire place, and wood for a fire, I'm going to ride up there to them trees, see if I can find some fresh meat for our first supper, here in the site of our new home." Thirty minutes later Ben heard a rifle shot. Grinning he hurried with his fire building chore. Ed returned with a small deer. While they dressed the deer, the women unpacked eating, and cooking utensils. In short order they had delicious deer steak, roasted potatoes, and coffee for supper. They ate, and marveled at their good fortune...so far.

CHAPTER 2

Ed made a cigarette from the small sack in his shirt pocket, walked a few paces away. Looking back, wondering...his lovely wife Helen, tall, golden hair, smiling green eyes. Ben's wife Jenney, with dark brown hair, deep brown eyes. Both strong, and healthy, embodying the pioneer type. Their sons sitting beside them. Joe, his and Helen's son. Russ, Ben and Jenneys son. Both tall and husky, for their age, thirteen now....did Ben and I do the right thing, bringing them to this wild, beautiful place?

Walking back, Ben asked, "What about Indians? Jud said this was Navaho country." Ed looked up, grinned saying, "I believe here comes the answer to your question." Ben turned to look were Ed had pointed, to see three riders coming their way. Even in the dim light, they could tell two were Indians, third an Army Officer. Ed hissed, "Keep your hand away from your gun, if they meant trouble it would have done happened." Ed and Ben stood, with their arm around their wife's waist, the boys beside them, waiting for them to approach. The Indians were two fine looking young men. Both were dressed in clean buckskin jacket, pants and leggings. These weren't just plain village Indians....As they were to learn... The Officer greeted them saying, "Howdy folks, I'm Colonel Fields, commander of Fort Wingate*, not far from here. Sorta off the beaten track ain't you?" Ed answered, "Guess we are. Planned to settle here, any objection to that?"

"Not from the Army. My scouts people, the Navaho might, and so will the Apache. But it's a little far south for them, except for occasional raids."

"How would you suggest we deal with the Navaho?"

"I can let my chief Scouts here, acting as your envoy, take you to powwow with their chief. I have found them reasonable people. Befriend them, and they wont bother you. In fact they will be a big help keeping the Apache away."

"Well thank you Colonel. Will you, and your Scouts dismount, have some fine deer steak with us?"

"Thank you no. it smells mighty good, but we must be getting back." With a salute , they turned, rode away.

*Fort Wingate was one of the many outposts built along the Santa Fe Trail protecting against Indian attacks on wagon trains going West to California.

CHAPTER 3

They accepted the Colonels advice, and got busy building a one room cabin for living quarters, until the ranch house could be built...the beginning of a fine Arizona ranch.

For the building site they chose a place way back in the valley. It was shaded by full leafy trees, and a cool spring emerged from under a large rock, trickling it's way to the stream. Trees were cut, and dragged in to begin building the ranch house. After weeks of hard work, Ed looked around one day and said, "By gawd Ben, the Circle W is going to be in business afore you know it. Does that name suit you?"

"Yep, just fine." Progress was slow, but at the end of five years, it had indeed grown into one of the finest ranches in the Arizona Territory.

The Circle W Ranch
1845

During that time, a growing town,.... Gila Springs, ... had built up at the intersection of the Gila and Santa Cruz rivers.

Helen took the buckboard into town for some needed supplies. On her way back she passed a Navaho woman and a young boy walking along the road. The woman had a large bundle on her shoulders. Her head was bowed, with a despondent look on her face. Helen stopped, waited for her to come beside the wagon. In halting language she asked, "Why you so far from village?"

"Husband bad, killed by soldiers. Go back to my village."

"You and boy get on wagon, go with me."

"Why go with you?"

"Would you like to live with me? I need a woman to help me. Big house, much work."

"You would let me do this?"

"Yes, I have young boy like this one. They could be friends."

"I come." She took her pack off laid it in the wagon, the grinning boy helping her up, she said, "His name Eagle. See good like the big bird. My name Maggie, in white mans words." Thus began a friendship that lasted many years.

Joe, Russ and Eagle became more than just friends, they were more like brothers. They were inseparable. Leaning to ride at an early age, they became excellent horsemen, cowhands and gun handlers. Ed and Ben spent many hours watching them, and laughing at them practicing their ...fast draw...

CHAPTER 4

With fall approaching, all the old-timer were predicting a hard winter this year. Ed decided to round up about five hundred head of cattle, drive them to the Santa Fe New Mexico market while the price was good. It would also help the winter feeding situation for the remaining herd.

He hired extra hands, and a salty old timer as the cook. The roundup began. Helen....as good a hand as the boys.... delighted in helping. and within a week, they had a herd close in.

While searching the North section of range for strays, Joe and Eagle spotted a covered wagon parked under a large tree, near a stream. Joe said, "We'd better ride over and see what this is about." Coming along side the wagon, Joe threw up his hand in a welcome gesture saying, "Howdy folks, you'll been here for a while? This is private range." The woman, working over the fire, never looked up. The man said, "Yes, we saw the sign back a ways. You the owner?"

"Yes, my family is."

"Someone back there in town told us, if we stayed up here near the tree line, it would be ok. Is it?" Joe laughed, "Just as long you don't cut out a fat calf for dinner." The man said. "I'd never think about it. I might try to buy one if I saw some one to ask."

"Where you folks headed?"

"To a place called Sundown. Are you acquainted with the place?"

"Yes, been there a few times, none recently though. You have relatives there?"

"Maybe."

"Why maybe?" Looking around he said, "The wife has just about got something to eat ready. Why don't you join us, and I'll tell you about maybe." Dismounting Eagle quipped, "Believe we will, something smells awfully good." The lady dished them up a plate of stew, and a cup of coffee. As they ate, Joe offered, "I'm Joe Wiseman, this is my partner Eagle. He's Indian, but don't be afraid, he won't scalp you." Laughing, Eagle swatted him across the back with his hat. The man replied, "My name is Jess Boudreau, my wife is Katrina."

"Where you hail from, your voice has a strange ring to it?"

"I'm Canadian, Katrina is Mexican." Joe shook his head, "How did two people from so far apart, ever get together?" Katrina answered, "I grew up in California. I had, what most people said, developed a good singing voice. I wanted to go East to study. Caught a ride with a family in a wagon train taking furs. Somehow I wound up singing and dancing in a saloon near the Canadian border. I thought Jess was so much different than most other men who came there. He was always polite, no crude talk, or pawing around. We began seeing a lot of each other, fell in love, and married."

"I decided I wanted to go back to California. Jess protested, but went along. Once there, He got a job in a winery, which he hated. We had a daughter, Anita. When she was one year old, nothing would do Jess but go back to Canada. My parents wouldn't see to us carrying a child so young, all the way across the country. So we left her with them until she was old enough, and they said, they would see she got to us. That time never came. Sparsely spaced letters told us little about her. At age sixteen, they wrote us she had left there, on her way to Canada, to find us. She never got there."

"About a year ago, we had word from a friend, who said he had passed through a place called Sundown Arizona. There was a girl that looked like me, sang like me. That was singing and dancing in a saloon there. We set out to find her. That's why we're here."

"Well folks, It's a pretty good ways from here to Sundown. Let me make a suggestion. About two months ago, my Dads brother, his wife and son went to a ranch near Sundown, to visit a friend of his wife, who was visiting her folks there. My Dad has received a incoherent letter from his brother, urging him to come, he needed help. Eagle here, and myself are leaving the first thing tomorrow to see what the trouble is. If you folks want to stay here another day or two, we will check on the girl. If it's her, we'll bring her back with us."

"How are you fixed for food supplies?"

"We could use some flour and coffee, otherwise we're ok."

"We'll have a couple of the boys at the ranch, bring you some things. Does this meet with your approval?"

"Yes, we can use the rest." Grinning he said, If you don't mind my team eating up your grass." Laughing, Joe said, "Well they look like they could stand a good meal or two, and the rest will do them good too. I'll have the boys throw in some grain with your supplies." "Well thank you Mam for the good meal. We best be getting back to the ranch." They mounted up, and with a wave rode away.

CHAPTER 5

Sundown, Arizona Territory

The next morning, Joe and Eagle headed for Sundown to check on both Ben, and the Boudreau girl. They traveled about ten miles, then stopped before nightfall, to camp by a fast -flowing brook. Helen had packed them a bag of sandwiches, and a tin of coffee.

As they ate Eagle asked, "What do you make of the Boudreau family? You know, letting their daughter go for seventeen years before they begin to worry about her?"

"Well it's hard to say. We don't know all the particulars about them. Maybe we will learn more about it, if we find her. But doggone it, I can't see waiting seventeen years before I went back for her. Well I don't think either one of us is smart enough to be mind readers, so let's get some sleep."

The next morning, after finishing the rest of the coffee, continued on their journey. Early in the afternoon, they pulled their mounts to a stop for a breather, on a knoll overlooking the town of Sundown. Shading his eyes against the afternoon sun, Joe remarked, "Well Eagle, Sundown is usually a sleepy little town. But not today, from the looks of the crowd gathered in front of the hotel. Wonder what's up."

"Don't know, but something has them all riled up. Let's ease on down and see." When they drew a little closer, they could see a tall pole with a cross arm. "By dam it's a hanging, that's what got them all stirred up," said Eagle. Passing a man at the rear of the group, Joe asked, "Who they hanging today?"

"Russ Wiseman."

"What for?"

"Murder."

"No wonder uncle Ben was calling for help!"

As they were talking, a man came around the building, leading a horse, with Russ in the saddle, a noose around his neck. A second man behind, carrying the coil of rope. When they reached the pole, the man threw the coil over the bar. Joe spurred his mount through the crowd calling, "You there, holding them reins, drop em' and you're a dead man! You behind, slap that horse on the rump, you're a dead man too! Now you with the rope, take that noose off the man's neck." The man handling the rope called, "Who in hell are you? This man's sentenced to hang." Eagle drew his gun and fired one shot. The rope parted against the cross bar. A second shot rang out a moment later. A man with a rifle came tumbling off the roof of a building across the street. Joe looked to the balcony of the hotel. A woman stood there with a shawl around her head and shoulders, smoke curling from the rifle barrel in her hand. He gave her a nod, rode in, reached across and cut the rope binding Russ's hands, pulled the rope from around his neck saying, "Move your horse over against the hotel." Raising his voice called, "Lady pitch that rifle down to him, and get down here fast." The three of them sat holding guns on the crowd. Joe called, "Is the livery stable owner in this bunch?" A man held up his hand, "Yes sir. Fred Rollings here."

"Fine, you run over to your stable, saddle the best horse you have. Make sure the saddle has a rifle boot on it. Make it fast."

The street was quiet. Just a mummer or a whisper now and then. Rollings returned trotting a fine looking bay mare, just as the lady emerged from the hotel. He handed her the reins, she handed the bag she was carrying up to Joe, and mounted. Joe asked, "What's the price of the horse and saddle? We don't take things without paying for them."

"That's ok Mr. Wiseman, we'll talk the next time you're in town." Joe stood up in his stirrups called out, "Where is the sheriff any way, why ain'he here. Don't he know all this is going on?" Someone called out, " He and the mayor left town after the trial, didn't say where they were going."

"Well folks, please go on home, clear the street. There will be no hanging today." Unbelievably a cheer went up from the crowd.

Joe said, "Ok we have some riding to do. Let's get started". Russ asked, "Where are we heading?"

"To uncle Ben's ranch. He and your mother has been absolutely worried to death about you."

"I'll tell you, you'll never know how happy I was to see your two ugly faces."

"We'll wait until we get you home, then you can tell everyone what happened. I for one am anxious to hear it."

"By they way, 'sharp shooter' what is your name?" Smiling she said, "Anita Boudreau."

"Well that gent on the roof top, was about to plug one or both of us. We have a surprise way of repaying you, but it'll have to wait until story telling time."

From time to time, Joe glancing around, saw Anita and Russ smiling at each other. Thought to himself I don't blame him. She is a very beautiful girl. Long shining black hair down to her shoulders, and a mischievous glint in those lovely dark eyes.

Riding up the lane to the house, they could see Ben and Jenny, standing out front waiting. One of the men had rode in to tell them they were on the way..

They could hardly wait until Rus had dismounted, before they run to him. Jenny with tears running down her cheeks, was first to reach him, hugging and kissing him, completely embarrassing a grinning Russ. Next Ben embraced him, adding to his discomfort. Then of course, they had ro embrace both Joe and Eagle. Russ introduced Anita. Jenny took her by the arm saying, "Everybody in the house. Angela...their Mexican cook, and housekeeper... has dinner ready. We'll eat first then talk. No talking about the incident at the table."

After they ate, and were all comfortably seated in the living room, Ben opened the discussion by asking, "Russ, what in gods name happened, that they wanted to hang you?"

"It started at a poker game, in the Sun Downer saloon. There was five of us in the game, sheriff Hodkiss, mayor Williams, Lester Crawford, Slim Dickins...the new house man and dealer.... and myself. The game had been going on for about an hour. The mayor was in a nasty mood. He was losing heavy. I had been keeping a eye on the dealer. His pile was to big for just being lucky, or a good bluffer, he was cheating."

"This hand had come down to two players. The mayor and dealer. The rest of us had folded our hands, too many raises for what we were holding. Four cards had been dealt. The mayor held two queens, and the eight of clubs up. Because of his raises, it was a sure bet he had the third queen in the hole. The dealer held two aces, and the three of hearts up. He was raising like he had the third one in the hole. He dealt the fifth card to the mayor, the seven of spades. Before he dealt himself the fifth card, he reached down, pretending to take a peak at his hole card. I reached across the table, grabbed his wrist, turned it over, and there was the ace of spades concealed in the palm of his hand."

"I had just turned his hands loose, when a shot rang out. The dealer slumped across the table dead. Every body jumped up, I was standing between the mayor and sheriff. The sheriff grabbed my arms, the mayor slipped my gun from the holster, replaced it with his, and began shouting, Russ has shot him. The sheriff pulled the gun from my holster, "Look, the barrels still hot. Give me some help. We'll take him over to the jail." Two or three cowboys standing around, jumped in to help...I don't hold any anger toward them. They really didn't know what had happened.... they pushed me into a cell, and locked the door. I heard the mayor say, "I'll send for the circuit judge to get here as quick as he can, and we'll try him for murder. That's a hanging offense here."

"He came in about a week later. A trial was held there in the saloon. I wasn't allowed to speak for myself, and no one spoke for me. It was quickly over, and I was sentenced to hang. The judge, sheriff and mayor left town, leaving two deputies to do their dirty work. It was about to happen, when Joe and Eagle rode in, and put a quick end to it. That's the truth, so help me God!"

CHAPTER 6

The room was quiet for a minute or two, before Joe asked Anita, "How did you come to get mixed up in this atrocious affair?" Looking at Russ and smiling, she answered, "Russ and I had become good friends. When he came in, we talked laughed, and had a good time. My agreement with Mr. and Mrs. Freeman, the owners, that I didn't have to dance with the customers, mostly drinking cowboys, ...who couldn't keep their hands to themselves.... But Russ and I danced some together. It caused a little ill feeling, but no one ever got nasty about it."

"The mayors ranting had people looking on. I was standing right behind Russ, saw exactly what happened. Russ didn't shoot that gambler, the mayor did, and I wasn't going to let them hang him for it. I was about to start shooting the two deputies, and try to make a get away, when Joe and Eagle rode up."

"Well the shot you did make, saved one or both of our hides," Joe added.

Jenney asked, "How did a pretty, wholesome girl like you, come to be working at a place like that?" Anita laughed, "Thank you for the compliment. I don't know about them things you said, but let me tell you'll about myself. I was born in Elkton California, to Jess and Katrina Boudreau. My Father is Canadian, mother Mexican. They had met just across the American border, where mother was singing, and dancing in a saloon. After a reasonable courtship they were married. Mother insisted that she wanted to return to California. Father gave in, and they returned. Father got a job working in a winery...which he said he detested. While he worked there, I was born. After a year, he insisted they return to Canada."

"When I was old enough to understand, this is what I was told. My mothers parents were adamant that I was to young to be carried across the country. When I was old enough they would see that I would be sent to join them. That time never came. They raised me as if I were their daughter. Seen to my schooling, singing lessons, every thing that I needed, or wanted. I know infrequent letters passed between them, but I was never informed on what they said."

"By the age of sixteen, I had developed a good singing voice. Just like my mother's I was told. One day passing the San Carlos hotel, I noticed a sign advertising for girl singers. I made myself up, trying to look older, went in, asked for an audition. I must have done well, for Mr. Gaston, the owner, gave me the job right off. I would sing in the dining room at the evening meal, for three hours every night. It never did interfere with my school work. When my grandparents found out what I was doing, and I convinced them that it was harmless, they came to dinner one night just to hear me sing."

"Things went well for about five months, and I was paid well, besides a few good tips. One night after my last performance, Mr. Gaston came to my little dressing room with making love on his mind. I fled that place in a hurry."

CHAPTER 7

"I decided I would go to Canada. I withdrew my money, ...I had saved every penny,... bought a ticket on the stage coach to St. Louis, not knowing what I'd do from there. On the seat across from me, sat a nice looking man and woman. In conversation, we passed names. Theirs were Carl and Ethel Freeman. They were returning from a trip to California to visit their son who lived there."

"When the stage stopped at a way station, I went out walking. I guess I must have been feeling good, because I began singing as I walked. When the stage coach started again, they told me they had heard me singing, and that I had a beautiful voice."

"Before the stage reached Sundown, they had convinced me to come live with them, sing in their saloon. They said I would be well taken care of. No harm would come to me. There would always be someone, who I would never see, close by while I was working in the saloon. They kept their word. There was never any real trouble until the angry mayor went on his rampage."

"Never got very far on my pilgrimage did I?" Jenney said, "Well my dear, you've had a time. Do you plan to continue on?"

"I'll have to give it some thought." Joe laughing said, "Eagle and I were talking to some folks just the other day, that said they had word from a friend, that had passed through Sundown Arizona, and that he seen a girl singing in a saloon that looked just like the woman we were talking to. You reckon that could have been you he was talking about?" Anita looked at him strangely, "What was the name of the people you were talking to, where were they?"

"I think they said their name was same as yours, Boudreau or something like that. They were traveling in a covered wagon, camped in our north range. Said they were trying to find that place Sundown.." Anita turned pale, putting her hands to her face. Joe leaned forward, took her hands saying, "I apologize. I was making a joke out of it, that was cruel. It was your parents. They were trying to find you. A letter from your grandparents had told them you had left, on your way to Canada to find them." Anita was softly crying. Jenney came over, put her arms around her saying, "Shame on you Joe Wiseman, that was indeed cruel."

"Anita dried her eyes, worked up a smile, "Well he did say he had a surprise for me." Ben yawned, "This has been some day. I guess you'll will be leaving tomorrow, so let's get some sleep."

CHAPTER 8

Unexpected Trouble

The next morning, when they were making ready to leave, Joe said, "I think it would be wise if Russ stayed under cover for a time. In fact I believe it best if he went to stay with us for a while. We're starting a cattle drive to Santa Fe when we get back, he could go along. That would keep him hid for a couple months. With the sheriff and mayor in hiding, I don't think there will be any repercussions for a while." "We sure will miss him, but I think you're right," responded Jenney. Ben agreed. She left to bring him a few clothes. After saying their goodby's they left for Gila Springs.

As they rode along Anita asked, "We don't have to go through Sundown do we? That was a deputy I shot off the top of that building. Some of his friends might want to get their hands on me."

"No we'll skirt around it, far enough they won't see us."

They didn't get to the by-pass point. Joe's horse, Kicker began shaking his head, and snorting, his ears standing straight up. "What's the matter Kicker, you don't want to go through Sundown either?" Anita laughed, "Why do you call him Kicker?"

"Well I raised him from a colt, he was the worst kicking thing I ever saw. Why he.....before he could finish, four horsemen rode out of a brushy draw up ahead, driving three steers ahead of them. Joe first thought they were cowboys rounding up some strays. As they got a little closer, the four "cowboys" gave a yell chasing the cattle away, drew their guns, came forward, surrounding them. A big rough looking, red beared man, obviously the leader, said, "Now you gents slowly unbuckle them gun belts, pitch them over there in that bush." No one moved. He drew the hammer back on his gun "now!" They slowly did as he said. When they had disposed of their guns, Red Beard said, "Now Reb here is going to lead in front, you'll just follow him in single file. We will be right behind, just ride along easy like, don't try any funny tricks." He motioned to Reb with his gun to go on, get in the lead. The terrain was rock strewn. First up grade, then down. They waded two small streams. Thick brush on each side, then tall trees. Russ couldn't place where they were going. He had never seen this part of the country, even though he had grown up not to far from here. Eagle was keeping a sharp eye out for land marks, which were scarce, because of the trees, and brush.

After traveling about an hour, they broke out of the brush to a flat grassy spot with large trees, and to their surprise, they saw a lean-to with a rock fire place, and a large black kettle hanging over it. Reb halted. Red Beard came around said, "Ok one of you dismount at the time. Reb and Jake here, are going to tie your hands, set you down by that big tree, and tie your feet, make you good and comfy..HAW!-HAW! The girl first." When they were all tied, the four walked a little distance away, began talking, and pointing to them. Shortly the fifth man appeared, carrying a arm full of wood. Evidently the cook. Red Beard called him over, spoke to him, again pointing to them. Then the four mounted and rode away. Directly, the cook picked up a pail, said, "I'm going down to the spring for a pail of water, don't you folks go wondering off." Cackling to himself went off down the hill.

Joe whispered, "Eagle scoot over here, get back to back with me, these are new ropes, I think we can get untied." He slid over, turned his back to Joe, and just a minute or two, was untied. He looked around, picked up a butcher knife, quickly cut them all loose except their feet. "Ok every body sit down like you were. Keep your hands behind your back, and watch me when that cackling roster comes back," quipped Joe. Ten minutes later, he came back up the hill humming to himself. When he set the bucket down, Joe tantalizing him asked, "Would you give a thirsty man a drink of that cool water?" He picked a dipper, hanging on a limb, filled it, walked over. "Here you are." And threw it in Joe's face. In a wink the cook was laying on the ground, flat of his back. Joe on top of him, with a haymaker to his jaw, put him out of commission. Eagle rushed over with his knife, had their feet cut loose in a jiffy. Joe pulled the cook up, unbuckled his gun belt, handed it to Anita. Then took some of the rope, tied him securely, both hands and feet, propped him against the tree. Laughing, Anita asked, "Where did you learn that trick?" Smiling he replied, "That's an old Indian trick. Eagle taught me, when we wrestled together, when we were kids."

Eagle walked over to the prisoner flashing his knife. "Ok chubby where did your buddies go"

"Went to tell the boss we had captured you guys."

"Where is your boss?"

"Over in Quincy, about ten miles from here."

"Know where that is Russ?"

"Yes, it's a regular outlaw hangout." "When do you expect them back?"

"In the morning they said."

"Ok that gives us plenty of time. Let's mount up and get away from here," Added Joe. When they were ready to leave, Joe said, "We'll be going now chubby, don't you wonder off any where, HAR! HAR!" imitating Red Beard.

CHAPTER 9

The Circle E Ranch

They left, following the trail they had come up on, mixing the new tracks with old. They emerged from the draw where they had entered. Russ asked, "Where are we going now?"

"Back to uncle Ben's. He has to be alerted to expect a posse tomorrow morning. Look over in that brush, see if our guns are still there." Russ dismounted, searched the brush, turned holding up their gun belts grinning, "I guess old Red Beard thought we'd not have need for them any more."

Ben and Jenney were dismayed to see them come riding back into the yard. They went into the house, where Russ told them what had happened. Joe explained, "We have to make some plans. I fully expect a posse in your front yard before noon tomorrow. I suggest you pull some of your boys in, put them upstairs with rifles. You go out to meet the posse, showing all the surprise you can muster. You will have make up a tale to answer their questions with. At daylight the four of us will ride up to that rocky outcropping, hide the horses, and get in a position we can see down here. If we think things are getting to nasty for you and the boys to handle, we'll rush back to join you. Now does anybody have a better idea, or any thing to add?"

"Well you boys finish your plans, Anita and I will go in and help Angela fix supper," quoted Jenney.

After she had gone Ben asked, "Why do you think they'll come here?"

"Russ has been convicted of murder...falsely of course....as long as he is free, the mayor is in danger of being found out. They have to catch Russ, and hang him quickly as possible. So I think they figure this is where he'll come to hide. They will look here first."

"I thought you said none of the people would join the sheriff's posse."

"It won't be a posse of citizens, but a posse of outlaws which the sheriff controls."

Jenney called them to supper. After they ate, and the kitchen cleaned up, Jenney began wondering how she was going to sleep them all. Joe solved part of the problem saying, "Eagle and I will sleep out in the bunk house."

"Don't play any poker with the guys, they're sharper than that dealer in Sundown. " Quipped Russ.

Come morning, everything was made ready for the expected posse. About nine, Russ called down to the others, from his lookout post, "Riders coming up the lane." Everyone found a position to watch. Seven horsemen rode into the yard in front of the house. Ben walked out to the top step smiling, called to the group, "Morning sheriff, what brings out here so early in the morning."

"Wanted to see that son of yours."

"What for?"

"Now Ben, you know he wanted for murder."

"I thought that all had been cleared up."

"Doggone it Ben." sputtered the sheriff. "You know your nephew and his Indian buddy, with the help of that girl, rode in there, shooting up the place, grabbed him away from my deputies, and rode off. I figure they had come here to hide."

"No such a thing sheriff. My nephew, his Indian buddy...as you say.... and the girl left, for Gila Spring yesterday morning. Russ left early this morning, said he had something to take care of, would be back this afternoon. That's all I know about it."

"You sure they are not here? You could be arrested for aiding a criminal."

"Sheriff you can search the place if you want to. It's just like I told you a while ago."

"No Ben, I'll take your word for it. I'll come back and check with you later." He turned his horse, led his posse away. Ben called to a cowboy standing by the corral gate, "John quickly, jump on one of them horses bareback, follow that bunch, see if they leave a lookout behind." He came back to report, "Sure did boss, and I've got his hiding place spotted."

Joe, watching them depart, waited until they were completely out of sight, nodded to his group, "Ok let's slip on down. Keep the house between you and the road." Ben was waiting for them out back. Laughing he asked, "Guess who was the posse leader?"

"I don't need three guesses, Sundown's efficient sheriff?"

"Right, and that big Red Bearded fellow you'll mentioned, was among them. Come on in the house, let's decide our next move."

Once inside, Joe explained, "Our next move is simple, we've got to get out of here quick. Is there a short cut across the mountain to hit the trail to Gila Springs?"

"Yes Russ can show you. You go up to the line cabin, then down the far side of the mountain, to hit the trail. It's kinda rough going, but it cuts miles off the distance."

"Ok gang, let's hit the trail." Jenney spoke up, "Not until you eat."

"Well aunt Jenney, it'll have to be a quick bite."

CHAPTER 10

The two cowboys working the north end of the range, Zeke Culpepper, and Curley Wescot, spotted them coming. Rode toward the cabin to meet them. "Russ, what in the Hell are you'll doing way up here?"

"We're looking for Old Big Boy....The mountain lion that had chewed up a couple steers....seen any thing of him lately?"

"No that rascal is too smart." They being isolated up here, didn't know about all the trouble that had taken place, and Russ knew they didn't have time to tell them. So he was passing off the mountain lion bit. The others waved, and they kept right on going.

It was slow going down the mountain, but once they hit the trail they picked up the pace. Joe dropped back beside Eagle, whispered, "Why don't you jump on ahead, get Anita's folks, lead them to the house. Explain to mom and dad about them. After seventeen years, I don't think it would be very pleasant for her to meet them out in the middle of nowhere." With a quick nod, Eagle tickled his mount with the spurs, and left at fast gallop. "Where is he going in such a hurry?" Russ asked. "He's going by the line camp to tell the boys we're back, and would be ready to start the drive in a day or two."

They rode into the yard an hour before sunset. Every body was out waiting for them. Anita set on her horse a moment looking. She had no idea what her parents would look like. Finally she dismounted, walked to the group, hesitated a moment, then said, "Momma? Papa?" Her parents stepped forward a bit, then they rushed into each others arms, tears streaming from their eyes. In fact there wasn't a dry eye any where. After a moment, Helen motioned for everyone toward the house, leaving them to themselves. After embracing for a while, with their arm about each other, they walked over to a bench beneath a tree, sat down to talk. It was well after dark, when Helen walked out to them saying, "I hate to disturb you, but won't you come on in, supper is on the table. Eat then we all can talk."

And talk they did. Jess and Katrina told their story. Anita explained what she had been doing, as much for her parents, as for Ed and Helen...leaving out about shooting that deputy off the roof, ...which Joe would tell them later... After a while, Joe took his mother aside, " Mom, we don't want to be rude, but we have heard all this before. If you don't mind, we three guys will slip out to the bunkhouse, and get some sleep. It's been a long day."

"Sure son, you'll go ahead." When they had said good night to everyone, Helen said, "Russ honey, we haven't had time to talk. It's nice to see you, and have you here. Maybe tomorrow you can tell us how Ben and Jenney have been doing."

"Well aunt Helen they have been fine. I have given them a lot of grief with this trouble I have gotten myself into."

"Well son, they will stand by you. That's what parents are for you know."

The next morning at breakfast, Ed said, "Clarence Elliston, want's to send a hundred fifty of his 'Circle CE' beef along with ours. He'll furnish three men to help with the drive. He should have them here tomorrow. We can start the drive the next day." "Great Dad, I'm really anxious to get started, and it will help to keep Russ out of sight for a while."

"Well while you'll are gone, I'm going to ride into Gila Springs, talk to sheriff Eddie Moss about bringing in a Federal Marshal. Eddie has no jurisdiction up there, he can't help us unless them dudes start nosing around here."

"Well Dad, something has to be done about that mess up there at Sundown, and Quincy. Maybe that is the answer. What's the Boudreau's going to do, did they say?"

"Yes, they're going on to California to see her parents. Anita ain't sure what she wants to do." Joe, seeing Russ had left the table, leaned over, and whispered to his Dad, "Don't be surprised at a wedding there before to long." Ed raised his eyebrows, shook his head grinning.

"Well, she is a nice girl and a pretty one also. Her parents seemed like nice folks, just have been mixed up a bit. I think everything is straightened out now. Katrina will be happy to be back in California with her parents."

CHAPTER 11

The Cattle Drive on the Trail to Santa Fe New Mexico Territory

The drive got under way early in the morning, they would be gone about two months. Ed and Helen rode out about a mile to a high knoll where they could watch them pass. They sat astride their horses, watching the panorama below them. It was indeed a sight to stir the blood in any Westerners heart. Ed said, "This reminds me of that day, long ago, when I sat on a knoll like this with Ben. Looking at this beautiful valley with the vision of thousands of cattle roaming through the lush green grass. It's a dream come true." After a while they reluctantly turned their mounts back toward the house.

The cattle drive moved along. Chuckling, Guss sent the three boys back to ride drag. Eating a little dust would make men out of them. But his intent was to give them experience. It took a good hand to ride drag. They moved along without any particular problems for about two weeks. Then one evening Gus came in to the chuck wagon for his supper. He dished up a tin plate of stew, poured a cup of steaming coffee, sat down with the others. He turned, looking up at the sky saying, "Boys I don't like the looks of them black clouds rolling in here. I feel like they are carrying a bad storm." ...He had no sooner said that, than a streak of lightening flashed across the far sky.... "When we finish eating, let's everybody don slickers, ride around the herd and try to keep 'em calm. If that thunder and lightening comes close in, a big crack of thunder and lightening is liable to make 'em bolt. ....Now in case they do, don't anybody ride in and try to turn 'em ... Let 'em run, don't want nobody hurt, ...ride beside 'em until they begin to slow down, then we can turn 'em, and bed 'em down where they stop."

They began riding around the herd, some singing softly. Then suddenly it came! A big streak of lightening that lit up the whole sky, with a booming crack of thunder, and off they went! Everyone did as instructed, but it happened any way. A frightened steer suddenly, trying to avoid one down in front of it, turned out from the herd. Joe riding beside the running herd, happened to be in it's path. The steer slammed into his horse, sending him flying out of the saddle, landing headfirst in a pile of rocks, knocking him unconscious.

The herd ran on about a mile before they slowed. Riders then were able to get around in front of the slow running herd. They finally started milling around, and then quieted. One by one they began to lay down.

When Joe temporarily regained consciousness, it was still pouring rain. The herd was gone. His horse was standing beside him. He somehow managed to climb back in the saddle. He must have pulled the horses head around, because he went directly across the churned up path the herd had made. Jolting in the saddle caused him to loose conscious again.

At daylight, the crew was up stirring around, hanging their wet saddle blankets on bushes to dry. With their bedrolls in the chuck wagon, still back where the stampede started, they had spread their saddle blankets in the driest place they could find....under a big tree...Guss looking around asked, "Where's Joe?" Looking at blank faces, "Do you suppose he went back to the chuck wagon for dry clothes?" Again blank faces. "Well it was dark when we bedded down, I suppose no one noticed who was here, or who wasn't." Looking up, he said, "Here comes the chuck wagon, maybe he knows something." When it pulled to a stop, they gathered around, as Guss asked the cook if he had seen Joe. He shook his head, "No, ain't he here? I ain't seen him since yesterday."

Guss said, "Eagle saddle up. We'll backtrack, he might be laying out there somewhere hurt." As they were saddling up, the cook said, "Boss I saw three head back there, trampled to death. If you can spare me some help, we'll go back and carve out some good steaks for supper." Before Guss could answer, two cowboys volunteered, and sure enough they had big juicy steaks that night.

But it wasn't a joyful meal. Guss and Eagle backtracked all the way back to where the chuck wagon had been parked. Turned around, came back, riding wide on each side, of the churned up path the cattle had made. Finally Guss said, "It's no use looking any further. That heavy rain last night, has washed away any tracks he might have left." They returned to camp with the bad news, and hope he would show up.

The herd was delivered to the stock yard, without any further incidents. They received a good price, just as Ed had predicted. The men were paid, and given a good bonus. Supplies were bought for the chuck wagon, and Guss headed them toward home... before they would blow all their pay, drinking, gambling and dance hall girls.

CHAPTER 12

At The Circle W Ranch

The Boudreau's visited with Ed and Helen a week before they left for California. Anita had asked Ed and Helen if she could stay with them for a while, until she made up her mind as to what she was going to do. Of course, she was welcome to stay as long as she liked, they were happy to have her.

Ed rode into Gila Springs to talk with sheriff Eddie Moss about bringing in a Federal Marshal. He rode down the street greeting people he knew, with a wave or a smiling good day. He tied his horse to the hitching rail in front of the sheriff's office. Walked up the steps, paused, asked a deputy sitting in a chair, leaned back against the wall, "Is the sheriff in this morning?" He took a puff on his cigarette, answered through a cloud of smoke, "Yep, go right in, he's got the coffee pot on, be glad to see'ya."

Ed walked in to find the sheriff pondering over a stack of 'wanted' posters. He looked up, saw who it was, stood up smiling, "Morning Ed, what brings you to our seat of law and order this day?" As they shook hands. "Want to talk to you about two gents not on any of them posters....but aught to be."

"Who could that be?" Ed filled him in on the incident at Sundown. The framing of Russ, his rescue by Joe, Eagle and Anita. Their capture by the sheriff's band of outlaws, their getaway, and all. "Whew, what a mess. But you know I don't have jurisdiction up there.?"

"I understand that. What I'm wondering if you could request a Federal Marshal to come here?" Eddie walked to the door, called out, "Pete, run over to Clarence Basset's office, ask him if he has time, would he mind stepping over here for a few minutes." Coming back to his chair he said, "Clarence is a good attorney, up on all that Federal stuff. We'll see what he has to say."

In a bit, Clarence walked in said, "Howdy Gents, shaking hands with each one, what can I help you with today Eddie?" He went through the story for him. "Where are these people now?"

"The mayor and sheriff have a headquarters in Quincy, the gang of outlaws probably hole up out in the rugged canyons and gorges to the west." Eddie said, "Do you have a description of any of them?"

"The girl says one of them is a big red bearded fellow." He thumbed through the posters, pulled out one, held it up, "Reckon it could be this one? If it is, his name is Alford "Red" Means, wanted in the New Mexico Territory for robbery and murder."

"Well that certainly enough to ask for a Marshal. I'll get a letter on the next stage to Frank Quesenberry, the Chief Marshal, give him a summary, and see what he to say, and get back to Eddie here, and he can contact you ok?" "Just fine Ed and Eddie said in unison." Clarence shook hands and departed.

CHAPTER 13

The Brenaman Ranch

When Joe regained consciousness again, he was lying in bed, a light shining in his eyes from a kerosene lamp someone was holding above his face. He tried to raise his arm to cover his face, but a hand caught it, a feminine voice said, "Well, you're finally waking up. Take it easy, you need rest." She sat the lamp on a bedside table, pulled the cover up to his chin, softly said, "Just relax, I'll be back shortly with some hot stew, and coffee."

After she left, he tried to raise up, but a splitting headache put him back down. He put hand up to his aching head. It was covered with a bandage. He lay there looking around as much as he could turn his head. It was a small room. Brightly colored paper covered the walls. What furniture he could see good, and well polished. The curtains over the single window were lace trimmed. It was undoubtedly a woman's bed room.

She returned with a small bowl of steaming stew, and a cup of coffee, and set it on the table. Came over saying, "I'm going to prop you up a little." Gently, she placed her arm behind his shoulder, pulled him forward, his head resting on her breast. That and the smell of her perfume made him take a deep breath. After she had fixed the pillow behind him, she pulled up a chair, reaching for the bowl of stew. All of this gave him time to look at her. She was quite beautiful. Lovely golden brown hair that fell to her shoulders, soft round face, rose colored cheeks, and laughing green eyes under long eyelashes.

She handed him the bowl asking, "Can you handle that, or do you want me to help you?" Feeling his sore face getting red he said, "I think I can manage." Before he took a bite he asked, "Where am I, who are you?" She replied, "My name is Stella Breanaman. You are at the Breanaman ranch. "Where is it located?"

"About five miles from Youngstown."

"Never heard of it. How did I get here?"

"Your horse brought you in. We had to pry your hands loose from the saddle horn." "How long have I been here?"

"Two days now."

"I know my head is hurt." Feeling his chest, "I must have hurt something in here."

"We had old doc Hines out here yesterday. He said you had a bad concussion, a nasty cut on your head, and a broken rib or two. He bandaged them up, said he'd be back today." She stood, looked out the window. "Matter of fact, he just rode into the yard."

Doc. Hines, a short chubby good natured man....looking every bit like a Doctor.... came in, deposited bag on the bed, smiling said, "Well my boy, did you have a good nap?"

"Yes, guess I did. The lady said I've been asleep for two days.."

"Yes, well let me look at your head, as he unwrapped the bandage." The bandage off, he felt all around with soft fingers. "Hum, them cuts and bruises look good. That big bump seems to be going down. You'll be good as new in a week or so."

"Stella, looks like you've been a good nurse." She smiled, "Well he's been a good patient."

"By the way son, what's your name for my records?" Joe looked at the Doc. Then Stella, with a blank look. Shaking his head, Doc said, "What I was afraid of. Temporary amnesia. It happens with a concussion like that. Nothing I can do about it. Sometimes the memory comes back quickly, other times.....he spread out his hands...it takes longer." He picked up his bag, looking at Joe said, "Son take it easy, rest all you can. I'll check back in a week or two. That is if you're still here," looking at Stella. "Oh, we'll keep him here if he'll stay"

CHAPTER 14

Guss returned with a tired crew, but happy to be home again, but sad at the same time, because Joe hadn't shown up yet.

Anita was especially happy to see Russ. They set out on the porch, laughing and talking, until Ed and Helen conspired to let them be alone for a while. Ed asked them if they would like to ride over to the "Circle E" with the Elliston's share of the money, the sale of the herd brought. They were indeed happy to so. When they came back. They passed the news to Ed and Helen, that everyone was invited over to Elliston's this weekend. They were giving a barbecue for friends, that were visiting them from California. Helen said, they would be happy to go, if Joe had come home by then.

At the Breanaman ranch

Joe's wounds were mending fine, but no sign that his memory was returning. Since he had been able to get up and move around he had not seen a man around the house. He asked Stella, "Where is your husband?"

"Oh, I'm not married."

"You run this ranch by your self?"

"Well not entirely, my foreman is a big help, and he has four men working for him."

"Where are your parents?"

"Mother died some time ago. My father was killed by rustlers about two months ago. They had been stealing our cattle. Dad decided to try to track them down, he got close enough to their hideout that he was shot by a lookout. His horse came dragging him home, one foot hung in the stirrup.?"

"Didn't he take any of the men with him?"

"No, he was too stubborn, and he was worried about my safety. You see, there is a big rancher on up the valley, Matt Clayborn who has been harassing Dad to sell our ranch to him. He also wants to marry me."

"Has he bothered you since your father's death?"

"No, I think he's waiting, thinking I'll give up and come to him. He'll be stumbling over his beard waiting for that to happen."

"Well you're a mighty strong lady."

He was feeling good enough to ride out looking for strays with some of the hands. They had instructions to watch him carefully, not let him stray off.

He spent a lot of time walking, laughing and talking with Stella. They were out walking one day, as they passed the corral. Jeb Crenshaw, a big rough looking cowboy was standing there. He stopped them asking of Stella, "How long are you going to keep that dude here."

"Just as long as I please. What is it to you?"

"You're getting to thick with him, and I don't like it."

"So what? We happen to like each other."

"Well you're my girl, and I don't like you flirting with him."

"What! You're girl! What ever gave you that idea?"

"You've been making eyes at me every time you saw me. Why I've even been thinking about asking you to marry me."

"Me marry you! I wouldn't marry you if you was the last man on earth. You get that out of your mind, and stay out of my way, or I'll ask Clyde to fire you." With that, she stomped off. When Joe caught up with her, she was so mad at Jeb, she was trembling like a leaf.

Joe said, "He has brass alright. But you must try to ignore and avoid him. But I'm afraid he is going to be trouble, especially for me. I could see the hatred in his eyes when he looked at me."

The incident was forgotten, and they continued to have their walks. Joe felt himself falling in love with this wonderful girl, but not knowing who he was put him in a quandary.

A few days after the disagreement with Jeb, they went on their usual walk, laughing and chatting. Suddenly, a shot rang out. A bullet passed through Joe's shirt sleeve, not touching the skin, and buried in a corral post. Quickly looking toward the direction the shot came from, they saw a rider hightailing out from behind the barn, through the pasture toward the woods. Stella grabbed his arm, fright and worry on her face, "Are you hurt?" Joe grinned, turned to show her the hole in his shirt sleeve said, "No but it was close. He didn't tarry long enough to see if he hit me or not. When he finds out he didn't, he'll try again when he gets the chance. It had to be our friend Jeb, don't you think?"

"Yes, I'm certain it was. But he's through around here, Clyde will see to that."

A month or so after he had arrived at the ranch, he was sitting on the top rail of the corral with Stella, watching a cowboy astride a bucking young horse, trying to break it for riding. It was bucking something fierce, suddenly off he came, he jumped up, grabbed up his hat, and climbed to the top of the corral. The horse stood there, throwing it's head, and pawing the ground. Joe looking at Stella saying, "You mind if I give it a try?"

"You think you're able enough?"

"Yes, let me try him on." Stella said, "No don't do it. You might get hurt really bad. How do you know you can ride a horse like that?"

"I just have that feeling." He jumped down walked slowly toward the horse, talking in a low voice, trying to calm him down. He picked up the halter, patted him on the neck, sill talking. He walked him a bit, talking and patting. He stopped him, quickly vaulted in the saddle, and away the horse went. He was fish tailing, around and around. Turned his head, tried to bite Joe's leg, then set into a real bucking stint. After a while he began to slow down, then began walking around the corral. Joe bent forward, talking into his ear, and patting his neck. He stopped him, dismounted, took the halter in his hand, started walking. The horse following him. When he thought the horse had calmed down enough, he took the saddle and halter off, laid them across the rail, then continued walking. The horse following him like a little puppy. He climbed out of the corral, receiving pats on the back from the cowboys that had been watching, and a hug and kiss from Stella. Suddenly he sat down holding his head! Stella ran to him, "What's the matter, your head hurting?" He shook his head, looked around asked, "What's going on? Who are you people?" Stella gasped, "His memory has returned! That bucking horse did it!" She took him by the arm, "Come on, let's go to the house, I'll try to explain everything." Once in the house, she led him to a chair, asked him to sit down. She knelt in front of him, took his hands in hers, and with teary eyes told him how he had come there, and what had been going on since his arrival. When she finished, she asked, "Can you remember now, what happened to bring you here?"

Joe looked at her for a long time, trying to organize his thoughts. Then he told her who he was, the cattle drive, the storm, and stampede. How the steer had ran into his horse, knocking him out of the saddle. He remembered climbing back in the saddle, and everything went blank again.

"It must have been s streak of luck, or fate, that guided me here. I must have been a heap of trouble to you folks."

"No, not at all. It has been as if you belonged here. After you got well enough, you rode with the boys, looking for strays. You and I took walks had fun talking. It's a terrible thing to say....she bowed her head...I'm almost sorry you regained your memory." "No, please don't feel that way. I've got this strange feeling I've known you a long time. Had we become very close?"

"Well it was like we were courting. We never embraced, or kissed, but I felt real close to you." He stood, lifted her up, put his arms around her, bent down, found her lips with a sweet kiss. Smiling he said, "We have now." She pulled his head down, kissed him long and hard. Put her head on his chest, breathing hard said, "I'm glad, I have waited, and wanted that."

Hesitantly she said, "I guess you'll be leaving us now." "Yes I guess my folks are worried about me. I'll have to go home to ease their mind, but...taking her hand....I'll be back for a visit now and then."

Joe went out to the corral whistled his horse over, took his saddle down from the rail saddled him, led him around to the front. Stella and Clyde were waiting to tell him goodby. Stella hugged and kissed him. He turned to shake hands with Clyde. He handed Joe his gun belt saying, "I cleaned the mud from it, oiled it and your gun, it should work fine." Stella said, "That reminds me." She told him about Jeb Crenshaw, the jealous cowboy, that taken a shot at him. She described him, and told Joe, "

"Watch out for him. We have no idea where he went. He might still lurking around, waiting for the chance to try it again." He hugged and kissed her again, and quickly mounted up, waving as he rode away, with the sweetness of her kiss warm on his lips, riding with him.

CHAPTER 15

Joe found he was farther away from Gila Springs than he figured. But he hurried on. It was late afternoon before he rode up the lane to the house. The place erupted with everyone wanting to be the first to greet him. But they made way for his mother, who ran to him, trying to stifle the tears, embraced him. "I've been worried sick about you. Afraid I'd never see you again. Where in the world have you been?" Hugging her said, "Why mom, I've been out courting." Holding him back so she could see his face, "Well she must have been some wild cat, from the looks of you. What did happen?" He broke away, greeting the rest of the folks. "Let's go in, I'll tell all of you the story." When they were all seated, Maggie brought in coffee for them, went over gave Joe a kiss on the cheek...her welcome home for him... then found a seat. She wanted to hear the story too. When he had finished, ...leaving out the falling in love part,... Helen said, "They must be nice folks. Maybe we can go to visit them sometime."

The Federal Marshal Art McMagee, was a six foot two hundred pound, muscular, square jawed fairly handsome man. His demeanor suggesting a man you didn't want to mess with, arrived in Gila Springs on Friday morning by stage coach. Checked in with sheriff Moss, who went over in detail...or as much in detail as he knew....why he was called out here. They talked till noon, when Eddie said, "Lets walk over to the hotel, have lunch, and if you are rested enough, I'll get you a horse from the livery stable, and we'll ride out to the Wiseman ranch."

"Fine, a good meal would energize me, and I'm anxious to get started."

As they rode along Art said, "I've never been out this way before. Sure is pretty country."

"Yes it is. Wait till you see the ranch. The Wiseman brothers as young men, with their families, and belongings in a covered wagon, settled here when it was wild country. Nothing here but the Indians, and the animals. Told about this place by a wise old wagon trail boss. He told them if he was younger, he'd grab it for himself. As the story is told. You will find them pleasant folks."

When they pulled up in front of the house, Ed came out to greet them. Introductions were made, and they were ushered into the house to meet the women folks, introductions were again made. They chatted socially for a while, before Ed suggested, "It's much cooler out on the porch. Would you'll like to sit out there, and we can talk about the situation?" Both Art and Eddie agreed.

Art asked the first question, "Do you have any new information, have you seen or heard from this outlaw sheriff and mayor?" Ed replied, "No, and that's puzzles us. They have to catch Russ to clear that mayors name. There has been no one poking around here that we know of. Our foreman was there, and would recognize them. He has rode around Gila Springs, and the area, seen no one." Ed surmised, "I guess the mayor and sheriff are holed up there in Quincy, hoping things will die down, since Joe, Guss, Eagle and Anita broke Russ out of the hangman's noose. Thinking setting Russ free, was all they were interested in and left." Art said, "I believe that's sound thinking. I think the first thing we aught to do is take a trip to this place Sundown, and Quincy, scout around a bit." Ed said, "You can borrow our boy Eagle. He's a pretty good scout"

"I'll tell you what. I'll have the cook, fix up some food. You'll can take a pack horse. It might take a day or two, to do your scouting. But first we are invited to a barbecue over at the "Circle E" a short distance away. Perhaps you would enjoy it."

"Great, I've never been to a real western barbecue, believe it or not."

"Then you and Eagle can leave from here. Is that agreeable?"

"Yes, indeed." "Sheriff will you stay and go along?"

"No, I'd love too, but I'd better get back." Ed asked, "Would you return his horse to the livery stable, and tell Jeff I'll settle with him for it's use, the next time I'm in town?"

"Sure thing, but I'll settle with Jeff."

Ed asked, "Is that your bag hanging on the saddle horn?"

"Yes, Eddie said you would want me to stay here while we worked." Ed called to cowboy standing in front of the bunkhouse, "Jim, would you bring Mr. McMagee's bag in from off that horse?" Ed took his bag went in, asked Jenny which bed room, took it and placed it by the bed.

CHAPTER 16

Scouting the Rugged Canyons and Gorges

They went to the barbecue. Art enjoyed himself. After packing away about all he could of the food said, "if I always felt like I do now. I'd never eat another bite." to the delight of the host.

Art and Eagle left on the following Monday morning, leading a pack horse carrying enough food.......Art jokingly said... to last them a month.

Riding along, Art asked Eagle, "How do you think we aught to handle this?"

"Well, I don't think there is any use to go to Sundown or Quincy. There is deputies in Sundown who can recognize me. We're quite sure the mayor and sheriff are in Quincy. When we get near there, we should branch off, head to the canyons, try to locate their hideout. When we have them all located, we can begin our roundup. Does that sound reasonable to you?"

"Yes it does. Only one thing, the area is a big place. Do you have a good idea where to start?"

"Yes, that is the reason I suggested the Quincy route. If they a rustling cattle and horses, ..as Anita says,... they would hide them somewhere opposite their headquarters." Art laughed, "Ok scout lead on."

Late that evening, they were near enough, Eagle suggested they make camp, get an early start in the morning. They found a grassy spot near a small stream, hobbled their horses, fixed themselves something to eat. Talked a while, kicked out the little fire, spread their saddle blankets, with the saddle for a pillow, got a good nights rest.

They were up and on the way, shortly after daybreak. After riding for two hours, they were in the dry washes and canyons Suddenly Eagle halted, raising his head, sniffing the air, looked at Art, "Do you smell smoke?"

"Yes, I was just about to ask you the same thing." Eagle looking around the high wall of the canyon said, "See that rock hanging out over the edge up there. I bet we can get a location from there. We'll have to leave our horses down here, find a way up by foot." They climbed the rock strewn, brushy slope to the top, crawled on their belly out to the edge. "There." said Eagle.... pointing to the right.... "Do you think that is a wisp of white smoke, or a cloud?"

"I'll go with smoke. With your sharp eyes, can you get an azimuth, and find it?"

"Well they say I have the eyes of an eagle...that's how I got my name....yes I think I can find it."

They got back to the horses, and with Eagle leading, they wound their way through canyons, until once again he halted, pointed to another high point. "Let's take a look from up there. We're going to have to be very careful, no sliding rocks. Let's take the horses around behind that big boulder, tie them in the bushes. If they don't happen to neigh, they won't be seen."

They took the long way around to the back side, the wall was less steep at this point. Still it was tough going. Pulling themselves by bushes, jagged rocks, any thing they could get a hand hold on, to reach the top. This time, Eagle motioned for Art to remove his hat, in order to keep a low profile, when they reached the edge.

There it was, a hundred yards away. Not only smoke, but as Art said, "It looks like a small town down there." They could see three or four men sitting around a rough table, evidently playing cards. One was over by the rock fire place. Art said, "I bet at times there is ten or more in there by the number of huts around the fire place. But it's my guess, that we are seeing all that is there now. Maybe there is more off tending to the cattle, if there is any."

"That's is what we're going to find out next." Asserted Eagle.

They moved back away from the edge, climbed down the tricky slope, went back to where they left the horses. Eagle said, "There has to be plenty of water, if they are hiding cattle up here, and it has to be somewhere below here." He led them wide around the entrance to the canyon the camp was in, found one running parallel to it. Moved down it apiece. Eagle held up his hand, pointing to an opening in the wall. It was arched like a natural bridge....a possible short cut from the camp, to where the cattle were.... Art shook his head signaling he understood. They moved on down. Eagle again held up his hand whispered, "I hear water, do you?" Art nodded that he heard it too. Down a little farther they found themselves looking down about fifty feet to a swift stream. They followed it, the floor of the canyon sloping steeper until it became almost level with the stream. A little farther it became a large pond, surrounded by a grassy meadow, where a good two hundred head of cattle, and a number of horses were grazing. Art was so stunned he had to sit down. After a minute he breathed, "This is hard for me to believe. All of this out here in the middle of sand and rocks. It's certainly one of natures beautiful tricks. You know it's hard to tell how long these thieves would have gotten away with this near perfect setup, if that angry mayor hadn't shot that cheating gambler."

They started to follow it further when two riders crossed in front of their view. Eagle asserted, "That puts an end to our scouting from this end. Let's backtrack, leave the canyons, go to the river, follow it until we find where this stream enters it. That will be the best way for us enter when we're ready to capture these dudes."

They did as Eagle suggested, found the stream, marked the place by two large trees growing on the bank of the river. Went back down river far enough to avoid discovery by the rider's watching the cattle, made camp for the night.

While they were eating, Art said, "I think we have all the information we need. We might as well head for home in the morning, put our heads together, come up with a plan on how to proceed from here."

CHAPTER 17

The Circle W Ranch

With Joe gone to visit the Brenamans, and Russ out on the range, Anita decided she wanted ti ride up to the pond, relax, and ponder about her situation. The reason she had stayed behind when her parents left, she felt she was falling in love with Russ, and she was quite sure he was in love with her. She wanted to assess her feelings thoroughly.

At the pond she dismounted, sat under a shade tree for a while, watching, and listening to the little falls. A desire sprung up to wade in the cool water. She rolled her pants up above her knees, kicking off her boots, and socks, waded out in the knee deep soothing water. Wading and splashing around, she felt better, and broke into a song

She neither seen, or heard, the rider come out of the brush back behind the pond. He sat watching, and listening to her sing for a minute or two, then he called out, "That's a pretty song. Are you singing it for me?" Startled, she floundered around in the water turning to see who it was. What saw turned her blood to ice. It was that big red bearded outlaw. He said, "Come on out sweetheart, we're going to visit an old friend." He was on the opposite side of the pond from her horse. She gauged the distance. She had just let the reins drag, didn't tie him up. She waited for Red Beard to make a move. He sat there laughing at her for a while. Decided he would have to wade in and get her. He started to dismount, when he threw his opposite leg across the saddle to the ground, and removed the other foot from the stirrup, she broke for her horse grabbed the reins, and the saddle horn, hit the horse with her knee, made a running mount, and rode away. Red Beard quickly mounted, splashed across the pond, and gave chase. Two cowboys making their rounds spotted them, and gave chase. Red Beard pulled his gun firing wildly back at them. The boys split, one to each side. He couldn't watch them both. One took his rope from the saddle horn, spurred his mount, got close enough to throw a loop around him, and jerked him from the saddle. Anita looking back saw what was happening, turned and rode back. Pete Armstrong, the roper looked in his saddle bag, got a piece of rawhide throng, handed it to Phil Jessup, his partner, to tie the captive hands. Phil said, "I've never seen you throw a loop like that before, been practicing?"

"Yep, thinking about Jining the rodeo." Anita rode up. Pete asked, "You know this dude, why was he after you?"

"Yes, I know him," She retorted. "He's one of the outlaws from Sundown. He said, "We were going to visit an old friend. His boss, the mayor, must have sent him to get me. Wants me for telling everybody he shot the gambler, and shooting that deputy." Red Beard, mad as a hornet growled, "You little snip, he'll cut your throat yet." Anita asked, "What are you going to do with him?"

"Take him to the house, Guss will know." They removed his gun belt, left the rope around his shoulders, put him back on his horse. Anita called, "Wait a minute, will one of you ride back there with me to get my boots? I was wading in the pond, when he rode up, frightening me out of my wits." Phil said, "I'll go. You just wait here until we get back." They rode off at a gallop, returned shortly, then they headed to the ranch house. Guss was standing at the corral when they arrived. Seeing Red Beard with the rope around him he exclaimed, "How in hell did he get in here past everybody, and how did he know Anita was at the pond? Well he did. I guess we're going to have to change our guarding some way. And Anita don't you venture out any more." She looked at the ground, ashamed she had caused the trouble. Guss said, "Let me saddle a horse, and we'll will take him in, turn him over to sheriff Moss."

When they rode up in front of the sheriff's office, a deputy sitting on the porch, jumped up ran to the door, called in, "Boss you'd better come out here and look at this." Eddie came out looked, "Where did you'll get that?" He asked. Guss explained what had happened. Eddie said, "Just a minute." He went inside, returned holding a wanted poster. He looked at the prisoner carefully, then the poster. He blurted, "You boys have captured a prize! That's Alford "Red" Means, wanted in the New Mexico Territory for robbery and murder! I'll lock him up, turn him over to the marshal. The poster says there's a reward for his capture, if there is, I'll turn it over to you guys."

CHAPTER 18

The Brenaman Ranch

Joe's visit back to the Brenaman ranch wasn't the happy occasion he had hoped for. Instead, he found things in a quandary. He rode into the yard, was tying his horse to the hitching rail, when Clyde came rushing out to greet him. Joe could tell by the look on his face, there was trouble here.

Shaking Joe's hand, Clyde said, "I'm sure glad to see you. We can use your help."

"Help doing what?"

"Stella is missing." The shock of hearing that, rocked Joe back on his heels. Clyde took his arm "Come on inside, I'll tell you what I know, and what I've been able to find out."

As they walked in, Clyde called to the cook to bring them coffee. When they were seated, and the coffee came Joe said, "Now just what has happened?"

"Well yesterday Stella took the buggy, went into town. Said she wanted to buy some material for a dress.... I think she was expecting you to come visiting sometime soon.... Well anyway, she hadn't returned by late evening. I was worried, rode into town. I didn't see any sign of the buggy, so I went into the general store, and asked about her. Mr. Gibbs said, "She was in earlier in the day. Bought a few yards of cloth... to make a dress she said....I walked out to the hitching rail with her, we chatted a few minutes, and I went back inside. A few minutes later I looked out the window, and saw her talking to two of her hands from the ranch. The next time I looked, she was gone."

"There wasn't any of our boys in town, so all I can figure it was Jeb Crenshaw, and one of his cronies. Of course Mr. Gibbs knew Jeb had worked here, didn't know he had been fired. I rushed on back home, thinking I might have missed her, I didn't bother to look for tracks leading away from the road. Then again she might not have come back the way she went."

Joe said, "If you'll let me borrow one of your horses, I'd like to give mine a rest, we'll take a ride back along the road, and give it a good check."

"Yes of course. There is three in the stable, all good horses, you can take your pick." Joe picked a young mare, saying, "She looks like a fast runner, if we have the occasion to move fast."

"She is, Stella delights racing her with the boys, and their horses"

CHAPTER 19

They rode along the road, one on each side. About a half a mile from town, Joe halted, motioned for Clyde to come over. He had dismounted, studying the ground. He said, "Looks like there has been some commotion here around a set of narrow rim wheels that could be buggy wheels." Clyde dismounted, examined the area, and said, "You see this. Mr. Brenaman had the blacksmith forge a "B" on each shoe he put on his horses. Same as a brand, he said." Looking closely four "B's" were plain where one horse had stood, and led off in a direction that would lead to Matt Claybern's big "C" ranch. Leading his horse, Joe walked out several yards in the direction the tracks were heading, studied the tracks again. Turning to Clyde, he said, "Three horses are going in this direction. The wheels are following the tracks with the "B", one set is beside the wheel tracks, the third set is behind the wheels, and traveling light, hardly making a track, no rider. It looks like one man has climbed in the buggy with Stella."

They followed the tracks, until they changed directions, leading away from the direction of the Claybern ranch, heading toward a copse of trees off to their left away's. They hurried in that direction. Riding into the trees, they spotted the buggy under a large tree. Clyde said, "I'll be dam, what do you make of this?" There was evidence of a struggle in the leaf covered ground. "It means Stella has put up a good fight before they got her out of the buggy and mounted. I think we can rule Claybern out.....for the time being... It looks like our friend Jeb, and who ever is with him, is who we'll be looking for."

Leaning as low to the ground as he could from the saddle, Joe was able to find enough hoof prints in the leaves until they broke out on meadow land. As they rode along, Clyde said, "This is Claybern grazing land now, it used to belong to Eli Henderson. He had started to the market with a herd to pay off a loan to the bank that they had promised to give him more time on. But was pressuring him for the money. The doggone rustlers hit the herd, while he was on the drive, scattered them out, run off what they wanted. All Eli was able to round up, didn't bring near enough for him to pay off his mortgage."

"Wouldn't the bank accept what he had to pay, and give him more time?"

"No you see, Claybern is an official in the bank, and had it foreclose on the loan, and he took it over. A lot of folks are thinking if he ain't the head of the rustlers."

"How does Stella stand at the bank?"

"She don't owe them anything. Mr. Brenaman would never borrow from the bank, but the time was coming he was going to have to. Claybern couldn't get to him through the bank, so he kept the pressure on him to sell.."

"If I recollect right, Eli had a cabin at the foot of them mountains. He liked to keep his cattle up there during the summer, bring them down for the winter. It looks like that's where these tracks are headed."

"Well it's going to be dark soon that aught to hide our approach." Thirty minutes later, in the dim light, they spotted the cabin. Smoke was coming from the chimney, and the dim glow of a kerosene lamp shown through the window.

When they got a little closer, Joe halted to study the layout. He said, "Let's swing a little wide, come in through those trees." When they arrived at the point, Joe wanted, they halted, dismounted, tied their horses reins to an overhanging limb. Joe again studied the cabin. Making up his mind said, "I'm going to slip up to that window to see what's going on. You go to the back, if there's a door, be ready to bust in."

Joe got to the window, carefully looking in. To his surprise, saw a third man, Claybern! And was in time to faintly hear him say, "Dam it... Jeb, I've told you for the last time, nobody touches the girl until she signs this paper. Then I'll have what I want, you can do what you want with the girl." Jeb drew his gun, pointing it at Claybern, "All right, get her over here to sign your dam paper now, or I'm taking her out, whether you like it or not." He reached over, grabbing Stella by the arm, trying to drag her to the table. She struggled, broke free. He grabbed her again, ripping her shirt, pulling her toward the door. She screamed, struggling harder. Clyde broke the back door open, Claybern drew his gun, Clyde shot him, then shot the lamp out. It immediately broke into flames. Jeb dragged Stella out the front door, right into Joe, who was heading there. He clobbered Jeb with his gun barrel, dropping him like a slaughtered steer. Clyde came out dragging Claybern who wasn't dead.....He was later to be sorry he hadn't finished him off....

Clyde brought Stella's horse from the hitching rail, leaving the others. She mounted, followed them to their horses. They quickly mounted, and rode away. Looking back they could see the flames from the burning cabin.

CHAPTER 20

The Circle W Ranch

Eagle and Art returned to the ranch, after finishing their scouting trip, anxious to get everyone together, and formulate some sort of a plan on breaking up the outlaw ring. They arrived right at supper time, and Helen wouldn't allow any conference to take place until everyone had eaten.

With Joe off visiting the Bernaman ranch, it left Art, Russ, Eagle, Ed and Guss to talk it over. Ed said, "Art you are the authority, you tell us how you want to do it, and we'll give you our full support and help."

Art replied, "Thank you for your confidence, and support. All the way back from our scouting trip, it kept running through my mind just what to do. In the absence of any law officials in the Sundown, and Quincy area, those people have been the most antagonized by the rustling of their stock, and the roughshod treatment by the sheriff and mayor of Sundown. We should recruit a posse, and deputize them, from that area."

"We have good enough reason to believe the sheriff and mayor are hiding in their headquarter at Quincy. It will be a simple matter to apprehend them, using no more than three men. My thought is that Guss, Russ and one deputy, could handle that very easily." Smiling he said, "I think it would grate on them heavily watching their hands being tied by those two." Laughing, Guss said, "I'm sure it would, having the man they framed turning the trick on them." Russ grinning, rubbed his hands together in anticipation of that act.

"We discovered a secret entrance to the hideout up there in the canyons, which will make the job for Eagle, Ed, posse and myself a lot easier also. We'll take enough men to drive out the herd of cattle and horses they have hidden in the most idyllic spot one could ever imagine."

"Ok, now I'm open for suggestions, or amendments. Guss said, "You talk like a army man." Art laughed, "You're pretty observant. I was a Captain in the Calvary before I resigned."

"I've said nothing about timing. Any suggestions about that?" Ed asked, "How long will it take to recruit your deputies?"

"Not long. When reach Sundown, I'll do that, then each party will be able move on to it's objective, ok?" A nodding of heads signaled ok. "There's one other thing, Anita tells me there's three or four of the sheriff's deputies that hang around the saloon. They'll have to be rounded up, placed in jail, with a deputy to guard them, before we leave from there. We don't want them, as a threat behind us."

"Back to the timing. This is Thursday. I suggest we arrive in Sundown Saturday morning. The reason being, there will probably be more men in town for us to choose our deputies from. I think we should leave Friday, make a dry camp that night, so as to arrive in Sundown by mid-morning Saturday. Is this agreeable with everyone?" A course of yes's concluded the discussion.

CHAPTER 21

Sundown, Arizona Territory September 1845

Friday morning, the men saddled their horses, led them to the front yard, where Helen and Anita waited to see them off. Helen embraced Ed, admonishing him to be careful. Anita, holding Russ's hand, threw her arm's around his neck, gave him a soft kiss, then blushing, moved over beside Helen. The men mounted up, with a wave, proceeded down the lane.

They traveled until dark, then made a dry camp. The next morning, as they were ready to start, Art asked Ed, "Are you acquainted with Carl Freeman the owner of the Sun Downer saloon?"

"Yes, we've been friends for years."

"Will any of the deputies, we'll be seeking recognize you?"

"Yes, probably, but not as the father of the man that rescued Russ, that day. Why do you ask?"

"I thought you and I would ride ahead, talk to Freeman, to see if he would point the known deputies out. If so, we can arrest them, lock them up in jail, before we ask for volunteer deputy marshals."

"Well Carl is a good man, I'm sure he'll cooperate."

"Ok, that's the way we'll play it."

The next day, when they were a short distance away from Sundown, Art halted them. He explained what he intended to do. He said, "You boys give us an hour, and then ride on in. Under that big shade tree looks like a good place to wait."

They rode into town, keeping an eye peeled for any hint of trouble. No one seemed to pay any attention to them. Stopping in front of the Sun Downer saloon, hitched their horses, walked right on in. They went up to the bar, where a smiling bartender asked, "What will it be gents?"

"Nothing, thank you. We'd like to see Mr. Freeman, is he in?"

"Let me check. He went through a curtain, returned saying, "Yes, he's in his office. Just go through that curtain, first door on the right."

They found Carl pouring over a ledger. Looking up, he recognized Ed. Stood up smiling, shook hands, "What brings you folks to this house of iniquity this morning." Ed introduced Art, and explained their purpose. Carl said, "Wait just a minute, let me look around out there. He came back shortly said, "There is four of them. The fifth one was killed when your folks rescued Russ from the hangman's noose some time back. The four are at a table over in the back corner. There is a fifth man sitting with them, the guy with the big white hat, ain't one of them."

"Is there a back door close to where they sit?"

"Yes, right beside them."

"Good, we don't want to disturb any of your customers. We'll take them quietly out the back door, no guns showing. Would you have someone to call that fifth man to the bar for something?"

"I'll take care of that." "Thank you much Carl. I'll buy you a drink some time, quipped Art. "By the way, do you know two responsible men I could deputize as guards at the jail until we return?"

"Yes, two brothers, Emery and John Barksdale. If you like I'll send for them, have them here when you're ready."

"Fine. I might want you to look over the ones I deputize, to be sure we don't have a bad apple."

"Be glad to."

They went out, walked casually down to the table, just as white hat was leaving. Art said, in a low tone, "We are U. S. Marshals. Will you gents get up, walk slowly out that door?"

"What you want us for?"

"Just get up and walk like I said. It will be explained to you." They got up, Ed opened the door, they marched quietly out.

Outside, one turned his head asked, "Where to?"

"Over there to the jail." Inside the jail, Art removed their gun belts, locked them in separate cells. As they left the jail, the two men Carl had recommended came up asking, "Did you want to see us?"

"Yes, but let me explain first. I'm going to swear you in as deputy U. S. Marshals to guard the jail here for a short period of time. I want you to understand you have the authority to shoot to kill anyone trying to force their way in here to take these prisoners out. Do you understand that, and could you do it if you had to?"

"You just let someone try it. They'll find out right quick."

"Ok, raise your right hand, and repeat after me." He proceeded to administer the oath. Then said, "I don't have a badge to give you, but I'll be swearing in some more men. I'll get a strip of red cloth from the store, to tie around your arms as a badge. Ok you can take over now. You don't have to stay inside all the time, you can set out here on the porch. But one of you must be here at all times." He shook their hands, and left.

CHAPTER 22

Art and Ed went over and stood on the top step of the hotel, Art pulled his gun, fired a shot in the air to gain attention. A crowd gathered around to see what was going on.

"Good morning, I'm Art McMagee U. S. Marshal. I've been called to this area because of the lax protection your law officials have been giving you. There has been rustling they have done nothing about, simply because they are the ring leaders of it. Killings committed by them, and blamed on innocent people. Women folks can't walk down the street without being jeered at by ruffians."

"Well, some of your good law abiding citizens wanted it stopped. I'm here to help do that, but I need help. I'm asking that ten men willing to accept the responsibility, step forward, and be sworn in as deputy U. S. Marshals, to help with the task. Before you step up here, you must understand there is danger involved. We have planned to keep that to a minimum.. Ok if you're interested, please step up here beside these steps."

Twelve men came forward. Art looked over at Carl standing just outside the group. He gave a nod of his head signifying the choice was ok. Art asked them to raise their right hand while he quoted the oath. He said, "I don't have badges to give you. But I'm going over to the store, get some red cloth to make a band to go on your arm, which will distinguish you as a marshal." A lady spoke up saying, "I'll get that for you." And went off in a hurry. Art called after her, "I'll need fifteen pieces twelve inches long, two inches wide. Tell the store owner I'll be in shortly to pay him." She waved acknowledgment went on.

Guss, Eagle and Russ rode up, dismounted walked up to join the others. Art said, "These gentlemen will join you." The lady returned with the strips of cloth, handed them to Art, "When I told him what this was for, Mr. Wade said there would be no charge."

"Ok thank you Ma'am." With Ed helping, they tied a band just above the elbow, of each man. "Now if you will get your horses, we are ready to go."

CHAPTER 23

The Canyons West of the Gila Valley, Arizona
September 1845

Art and Eagle led the posse up the river to a point they figured was a safe distance away from the entrance to the hideout, by dark. Art halted them. "Ok we figure daylight would be the best time to catch them off guard, so we're going to camp here until then. The reason we stopped back here is, the day we scouted the place, there was two guards just up the canyon a ways guarding the cattle and horses, they had rustled, and was hiding them here. We think they go back up to the camp after dark. Also that day we could see five men at the camp. Now there might five or fifteen, we're not sure. That's the reason for the caution. We can't have a fire, and no smoking. So let's spread our saddle blankets and get a little sleep. If you have anything to eat in your saddle bags, go to it. If not swallow real hard for your supper"....this drew some laughter, a good sign they were relaxed....

Just at daybreak they were saddled up and ready to go. Art warned, "Go slow and easy through the cattle. We don't want them up making a lot of noise. Watch for my signal, when we break out into the camp area, ride in fast, firing in the air, and yelling, to create all the confusion you can. Ok let's go."

They eased their way through, the cattle didn't pay much attention to them. When they passed under the arch Art gave his signal, and they rushed in firing, and yelling like a bunch of Comanches. Men erupted from their huts in all manner of dress. The ones carrying guns made no attempt to use them, the confusion was so great. There were only six of them.

When things quieted down, Art called out, "We're U. S. Marshals. You with guns pitch then out in front." He motioned to one of the deputies to gather them up.

Art continued, "One deputy to each man, take him inside to put his clothes on, search the hut good. Two of you go back to that rope corral, saddle a horse for each one. If there are any extra chase them down the canyon to the cattle. One man cut up that tent rope, in lengths to bind their hands with." The search netted a small sum of money stashed in various places. Ed placed it in his saddle bag. He would turn it over to the proper authorities later. In short order they were ready to move out. Art said, "Let's set fire to them huts. ....They're probably full of bed bugs any way...." They left out, leaving the huts burning. Art in the lead. A deputy leading a prisoners horse, the rest following.

When they reached where the cattle and horses were, Art said, "We want to drive these animals out, and take them with us. We can drive them to a ranch close by, post a notice in town where they are, and owners who have lost stock can come and cut out what belongs to them. Anybody know where there is a ranch close by?" A deputy spoke up, "That would be the Brenaman ranch."

"Anybody know where it is?" Guss answered that he did. "Ok Guss, you take charge, ask for volunteers to help you, and take them there. We'll head on to Sundown with the prisoners." Guss knew that's the ranch Joe's friends own. Maybe he's still there.

When they neared Quincy, Art halted them smiling asked, "Eagle you Russ, and one deputy want to ride to Quincy, pick up the mayor and sheriff, and bring them along?"

"It'll be my pleasure," A grinning Russ retorted.

Quincy Arizona

They rode in to town, stopped at the hotel. Went in asked the clerk for the key to the mayor and sheriff's room. He blurted, "I'm not allowed to give keys to someone's room!"

"We're U.S. Marshals, if you don't want the door knocked down, you'd better hand over the key, and be quick about it." He reached under his desk, Eagle grabbed his shoulder, "I said key, be sure that's all you bring out." He came out with the key, nervously handed it over, "It's room number five, first door on the right from the top of the stairs." "Now you stay just where you are, and don't make any noise." They eased up the stairs, found the door, slipped in the key, flung it open. Both men jumped up, the mayor swearing, "Who in the hell are you, don't you knock before you enter someone's room?" Then he spied Russ, "What's that killer doing here, he belongs in jail.?"

"Well we're here to swap places, put the real killer in jail, so the innocent one can stay free."

"Now you look here, you have no authority to come in here like this." Looking at the sheriff, "You going to let them get away with this?"

"A marshal's authority tops mine. Best we go along, let our attorney handle it."

"Eagle said, "Deputy you pick up them gun belts, and we're going to walk out of here real natural like. Russ you in front, you two behind him." He reiterated, "Remember real natural like, or it'll be a short walk,"

Once outside, Eagle said, "Deputy, you bring our horses over to the livery stable there. We'll round up mounts for these two." At the stable, while their horses were being saddled, their hands were tied. Laughing Eagle said, "Just so you can't pick your nose." Their horses were saddled, led outside. They mounted up, with Russ and the deputy leading their horses, set out to Sundown.

The Brenaman ranch

As they neared the Brenaman ranch, ...with the captured herd,.... a rider from the ranch spotted them, and rode over to see who they were. Guss told him, "They are stolen stock. We have orders to bring them there until the rightful owners can be notified."

"Would you go tell the owners of the ranch, and find out where they want them pastured."

"Yes sir." And raced off.

Joe coming to meet them, was surprised to see it was Guss leading them. They both dismounted laughing, shook hands. Joe asked, "Guss where in the world did you get these critters, and why are you bringing them here?"

"If you tell these boys where you want them put, I'll tell you all about it."

"Jack, ...the man that rode back with him, ...take them up near that burned cabin. Then bring those boys back to the house." 'Yes sir."

"Come on Guss, let's go on in."

At the house, Joe introduced Stella saying, "Miss Brenaman is the owner. Taking over after her farther was killed tracking the outlaws down that had been stealing their cattle. He got to close, and was shot by a lookout." Shaking her hand, Guss in a pathetic voice said, "Well Miss Brenaman, you won't have any more trouble from them. If you'll give me a cool glass of water, I'll tell you'll why."

"Sure. When have you eaten last?"

"Miss I can't remember. But my belly says it's been a good while."

"Well we'll see to that too." Joe added, "He has four men with him that probably have growling bellies too. They'll be here by the time Angie can have dinner ready."

"Guss you have time to tell us the story before we eat."

"Well you know about Art, the U. S. Marshal your father had brought in. He was at one time, a Captain in the Cavalry. He and Eagle went out to the canyons, scouted the place, found their hideout, and all these cattle you just saw. He organized a regular army campaign, and we went in there and cleaned that rat's nest out. I guess by now, Russ and Eagle, with one deputy, have the sheriff and mayor in tow to put an end to their dirty work."

"I bet it gave Russ some kind of pleasure to be the one to help nip the mayor and sheriff."

"You bet," Voiced Guss laughing, "I can hardly wait to hear about it."

"The marshal might have another rat's nest to clean out. There is a tyrant here in Youngstown ....if he's still alive....just as bad as they were." Joe proceeded to tell him about Stella's kidnaping.

The boys arrived from pasturing the cattle, just as supper was being placed on the table. When they had finished eating, Guss said, "This has been nice, and we thank you for the good meal, but I guess we had better get along. When are you coming in." Talking to Joe. "I don't know. With this trouble going on here, I believe I'll stay around for a while. Just tell the folks I'm ok."

CHAPTER 24

Sundown Arizona

Art arrived with his prisoners, placed them in jail dismissed the deputies, and waited for Russ and Eagle. He and Ed went over to the hotel, ate a welcome meal.

Guss and his men, appeared first, just shortly before Russ and Eagle with their two prisoners.

Art debated on what was the best thing to do with the mayor and sheriff. He decided it best to take them to Fort Wingate for safe keeping. He talked it over with the others, and they agreed

Ed, Guss, and Russ would go on to Gila Springs, he and Eagle would escort the sheriff, and mayor to the Fort, then return to the ranch.

At Fort Wingate, they left the prisoners under guard until they went in and talked to Colonel Martin....Colonel Fields had retired.....Colonel Martin had known Art when he was a Cavalry officer. They talked a while about old times, before the Colonel asked, "What bring you here today, want to re-enlist?" Art laughing said, "No, I doubt they would have me back, if General Foley is still out here. What I wanted to talk to you about is, I have two prisoners out there, and one more at Gila Springs, I would like help, to escort them to the prison in Phoenix. Two of them are murders, the other an accomplice."

"How soon do you want to leave?"

"Well, I have to go to Gila Springs first. Say about a week?"

"Ok, when you're ready come on back, we'll take care of it."

"I'm sorry, I got so caught up in old times, I forgot to introduce my partner here. This is Eagle...his only name....one of the best scouts in Arizona."

"Pleased to meet you. Shaking hands, "You wouldn't be interested in coming to work for the army would you?"

"No sir, I'm perfectly happy just where I am."

"Well some like it some don't uh Art?"

"Yep that's right." Art, shaking hands with the Colonel said, "See you in about a week." They went out, saw the prisoners had been locked up, departed for the ranch.

The Brenaman Ranch a Week Later

Joe, Clyde and Stella were sitting on the porch just after dark, when the man riding night duty with the herd, came riding fast into the yard. Pulling his mount to a sliding halt exclaimed, "I just saw a group of riders headed this way, carrying torches." Joe said. "Clyde quickly, get the boys out of the bunkhouse. Tell them to bring rifles." When they came he said, "Up stairs, cover all the windows. If they attempt to set fire to the barn or house, shoot them off their horse. Don't allow anyone of them to throw a torch."

Joe went in, put on his gun belt, brought Stella her gun, Clyde was wearing his. They set back and waited. It wasn't long before The riders appeared. Claybern...his shoulder showing a large bandage....was leading. They rode up in front of the house. Claybern called out, "You tried to burn me up, now it's your turn. I'm personally going to throw the first torch." He raised up in the saddle, lifted his good arm to throw. Joe drew his gun, fired at him point blank knocking him out of the saddle, his torch falling beside him. Jeb was next to try, Clyde shot him out of the saddle also. The rest threw their torches to the ground, turned their horses, and raced away.

The men came down, went out with Clyde, to inspect the two victims. After looking at them closely, Clyde called back to the porch, "They are both dead." Joe went out, Clyde stood saying, "What do we do with them."

"Load them across their saddles, lead the horses out close enough, they will find their way home. Then we wait and see what happens."

The next afternoon, the sheriff and two deputies from Youngstown appeared in the yard, in front of the house. Joe, Clyde and Stella went out to meet them. The sheriff looking around, seeing the burnt out torches said, "Looks like you folks had a bit of trouble here last night. Just what happened?"

"Claybern and his gang rode in here with flaming torches, with the intent of burning us out. He and Jeb Crenshaw made a run at the house with raised torches, and we shot them. The rest threw their torches down, turned and left."

"Well, Claybern's foeman rode in this morning, wanting to swear out a warrant for your arrest. The judge wouldn't grant it until I came out to investigate. I will report that it was an act of self defense, to save life and property. There will be no warrant. The incident is closed. It's sad, but those things happen. Well good day." He turned and rode away.

Joe said, "What do you make of that?" Clyde hearing it all said, "Claybern held both the judge and sheriff under his thumb. They are glad to be rid of him."

"Well, with this bunch cleaned up. And the ones at Sundown, and Quincy, this territory is becoming a better place."

"Amen to that." Clyde responded.

The Circle W Ranch

Things were beginning to return to some seemliness of normalcy. Art, his work finished here, was making preparations to leave. Eagle would ride with him to Gila Springs, where he would pick up Red Beard from Eddie Moss's jail, and to Fort Wingate, where would get the mayor and sheriff, and a military escort to Phoenix with them. Eagle would then return home with his horse.

With the danger taken care of, Russ and Anita were making preparations to leave for Sundown and his home. Anita couldn't thank Helen and Ed enough for taking such good care of her. Helen took her aside for a woman to woman talk. Helen said, "Honey I'm not prying, but I know you and Russ have become very close, if there is a wedding, we want to be invited." Anita laughed, "He hasn't asked me yet....holding up crossed fingers... I may have to do the proposing."

CHAPTER 25

Gila Valley Southwest Arizona Territory 1848

Ths ensuing years found Joe and Stella, Russ and Anita married....no children yet... The ranches grew and prospered. The Towns of Sundown and Quincy had elected new and responsible officials. Combined with Gila Springs, made an envious community of towns there in the Southwest corner of the territory.

During that period, the three ranches, the "Circle W"...Ed and Helen Wiseman... the "Circle B"...Ben and Jenny, Russ and Anita Wiseman.....the "Bar- J.S."....Joe and Stella (Brenaman) Wiseman, combined to drive the largest herd of the time to market. Two thousand head were assembled at a central location, driven to the Santa Fe market.

The fact that accentuated the uniqueness of it was, the women participated. They all were excellent horsewomen, loved ranch life. Worked the roundups with the men. Helen and Jenny expressing, "This would be the last 'Hurrah' for them. They were getting too old." Of course Anita and Stella could carry on for a good while yet.

The Gila Springs Gazette
Headline
GOLD DISCOVERED
IN CALIFORNIA

Ed, returning from a trip to Gila Springs, rushed into the house waving the paper, excitedly calling, "Look at this!...gold found in California! It says here that nuggets as big as hen eggs lying around everywhere. You can pick them up in a basket."

"Pshaw," said Helen. "You're getting all worked up over a fairy tale. There's been gold out there all the time. Back when I was working in dad's store, old prospectors came in with little bag's of gold dust they said was panned out of mountain streams. They wanted to spend it buying a grubstake, to go back looking for more. Maybe someone has found a little more than usual, and making a big ballyhoo out of it.."

As it turned there was a big strike. People were pouring in, hoping to hit it big. Wagon trains, single wagons, people with pack horses, all trying to cross the Rockies before winter caught them. Not all were after gold. Some were looking for a new life . From that came many stories of disaster.

The Circle W Ranch
September 1848

To Ed and Helen's astonishment, a covered wagon pulled into their yard one afternoon. The occupants were even more astonishing.

When Ed and Helen went out to see who in the world could be visiting them in such a rig. Found Joe, Stella, Russ and Anita, climbing down smiling asking, "Can you folks put up some weary travelers that have lost their way?"

"For heavens sake, what are you'll doing with that thing, where do you think you're going?"

"We happen to be on our way to California. Haven't you heard there's gold out there? We are on our way to claim our part."

"You mean Anita and Stella are foolish enough to let you two men go traipsing off on such a injudicious trip?"

"No of course not, they are going too."

"What! You can't be serious! Why ever killer, thief, robber, and scum of the earth conjugate in those mining camps. No place for women to be."

Anita spoke saying, "We won't be going to a mining camp. We're going to enlist my grandfather as a guide. He trapped, and hunted those mountains as a young man. I believe he could lead us to a place isolated from all the hubbub, build our own camp, ...so to speak...."

"When do you'll plan to leave on this dubious escapade?"

"If you will let us camp here for a week, while we stock up on supplies, then we'll be on our way."

"Gracious me, of course you can camp...as you call it...just as long as you like. What kind of supplies are you talking about?"

"Mining equipment, we're thinking those things will be hard to find around there." Ed hadn't said a word while the banter was going on, now said, "I wouldn't invest too heavily on picks and shovels yet. When you get there, find out what you need, send back for it. I think it would all depend as to what Anita's grandfather decides. If he is not interested, or don't think he knows about such a place, you had better turn tail. And head back home. Don't go floundering around out there in a place you know nothing about. As your mother said, the danger is too great."

Joe said, "Well, Mom and Dad, there's four, ...five including Eagle who had already stated he was going too ...grown people here, and I know the parents of them didn't raise any foolish children. If at any point, we feel we're acting foolishly, and the danger is too great, we'll do just exactly that."

They spent a week obtaining the supplies, seeing to the maintenance of their wagon. Ed had looked it over and suggested, "If you don't grease them creaky wheels, you never get off the ranch. I don't see how you made it this far without losing a wheel or two.."

"Wiseman's luck," quipped Joe.

CHAPTER 26

Elkton California
September 1848

With Anita guiding them the one wagon ...wagon train.. Pulled to stop on the road in front of the Alverez home. They came out to see what was going on, and were surprised to see Anita jump from the wagon, run to embrace them. Grandmother Alverez, tears forming in her eyes, hugged her granddaughter saying, "How wonderful to see you again." Looking over her shoulder she asked, "Who are your friends?" Russ had climbed down by then. Anita took his hand, smiling broadly said, "This is my best friend, and also my husband." With an incredible look on her face grandmother said, "When did this happen? Katrina and Jess were here, said they found you, and that you were well and happy, but nothing about you being married." Turning to Russ said, "Well, looks like you found a fine young man." Walked over embraced a smiling, but embarrassed Russ.

Anita continued the introductions by saying, "These is really my best friends, Stella and Joe Wiseman, and Eagle. Joe and Russ are cousins, and Eagle is their adopted brother. They grew up together, and are inseparable. I'll have to tell the story of how we meet." Juanita Alverez went to, and embraced them also. Grandfather Steve had been standing by, moved in to embrace Anita, sizing up Russ, ...deciding he liked what he saw, ... gave him firm hand shake. He then embraced Stella and Joe, and again,....liking what he saw...gave Joe the same firm hand shake. He studied Eagle a moment, decided here was a man you wouldn't want to mess with, then gave him that firm hand shake. Juanita, taking Stella and Anita between her said, "For lands sake, let's don't stand around out here, lets go inside. I bet you people are starved to death. We'll find something to eat, then do our talking."

Steve announced, "We had better take this wagon over to the livery stable, park it there for the time being, get these horses in so they can be watered and fed." He rode over with Russ, Eagle and Joe to make the arrangement for them. As they walked back he said, "I got a feeling you fellows has prospecting on your mind. Do you know anything about it?"

"No, perfect greenhorns."

"You must be very careful, you could run into all kinds of trouble. There's some mighty slick hombre's out there."

"Anita is of the opinion you could lead us to a good place, away from the crowded area."

"Well, I have wanted to give it a try, if I could find the right partners."

"Years ago, when I was hunting and trapping, I found cold streams cascading down to ponds. I collected some handsome mink and beaver hides there. I also found specks of gold in some of the shallow places. Never thought much about it. In fact I still have a small bit in a beaver skin bag in the trunk up stairs. I'll show it to you boys tonight. Now that this gold craze has erupted, I have been giving more thought to it..... Well here we are, we'll talk some more about it tonight."

The subject was brought up again after dinner. Steve described the risks one must take in getting to where you might find the gold, then asked, "Do you girls really want to challenge those mountains with these fellows?"

"That's what we're here for. Women turn up in unusual places, why not on a mountain?" "Well, that's what's making the west great. Women, and men braving the dangers. I hope we never loose that pioneer spirit."

"I haven't asked, and you haven't volunteered to say, where is Mom and Dad?"

"They stayed around here for about a year. But your Dad got restless again, and they headed up north towards the good farming land. We've had several letters from them. Seem like they're doing fine. Maybe Jess has found his calling."

Prospecting was discussed some more. Steve went up stairs, returned with the little bag of gold dust he had mentioned. He poured some out on a plate, "This is what it looks like in the dust form, found mostly in the streams. But it has to come from larger pieces buried in the rocks." Joe asked, "Why didn't you ever spend it?"

"Well, that is just a small amount in dollars and cents, I thought I'd save it for a souvenir."

"If you'll are serious, we will start gathering the tools we will need, and give it a try. We'll need more wood working tools than mining tools."

"Why wood working tools,? Queried Russ."

"I don't suppose you want to live out in the open do you? We must build some sort of shelter. And there will be a sluice trough with baffles to catch the small grains of dust when the rocks are washed, some kind of crude furniture like table, chairs etc. I suggest we take buffalo hides for bedding." Juanita exclaimed, "Surely you don't think you're going to be there that long. You're talking about a permanent residence!" They all laughed. "Even if it's only three months, we'll need a shelter of some kind," Retorted Steve. They bantered back and forth until late in the night. It finally ended when Juanita said, "Well I hope you're taking me a rocking chair.". ....she had no intention of going..... With a good laugh, they went to bed.

CHAPTER 27

Bald Mountain California 1848

It took them two weeks to round up their supplies and two burro pack animals, before they were ready to go.

Joe, walking up the steps to the general store for food supplies, met an old timer,

coming out. .....grey headed, a floppy old hat that looked like his burro had used it for a bed.... Holding up two cans of peaches, A toothless grin spreading across his craggy face he said, "Peaches, lordy how I crave 'em when I'm back in them mountns'. It's hard to find somethin sweet. The bars grab all the honey within reach." Joe watched him walk over to a shade tree, where his burro was tethered, set down, pulled a knife from his boot, cut the top out of one can, speared a slice of peach, placed it in his mouth, leaned back sighing, his eyes shut, enjoying the savor of it. After he had another slice, he speared one, held it up to the burro. She gobbled it up, enjoying it as much as the old timer did. Smiling, shaking his head, Joe continued on in the store.

When he came back out, began tying his purchase to the rack on one of the burro's back, a call of young man! young man! caught his attention. Looking over, he saw the old timer waving to him. He walked over, bent down on one knee in front of him, waiting until he and the burro finished the can of peaches.

Wiping his mouth with the back of his hand he asked, "Goin' prospectn'?"

"Thinking about it."

"Ever dun' 'eny?"

"No, just a greenhorn trying my luck."

"By yourself?"

"No I have three partners, all but one are greenhorns too."

"Well I liked you when we met over thar. Said to my self, "Now thar's a young man worth his salt. I'm going to tell you a secret. Ain't no body nos bout it but me and old Nellie here."

Looking around to see if there was anybody close he began, "The last time I was in the mountns' trappin, by pure chance, I come across this trail. It'd grown up so's you could barely see it. Well me and Nellie, she's sure footed as 'eny goat, followed it for maybe a mile to a steep drop of maybe twenty feet. I tied a rope 'round Nellie's middle, wrapped the other end around a tree, letting the rope slip a little at a time, I gradul let her down. Course all I had to do was slide down on my rear end. On about half mile further, we found the purtiest place you'd ever see. I made camp thar, beside a stream that was jumpin' 'live with mink and otter." Opening the second can of peaches, He continued, "Well you're prospectin', not trapping."

"What I'm tryin' to get at is, I found gold, lots of it in 'em streams. I only panned some to buy my next grub stake with. Now what I'm talkin' about is, if thars gold dust in 'em streams, thar hast to be plenty more up thar in 'em the rocks, big pieces I'm talking 'bout." Reaching in his pocket, "Now I have made a map,...you can read can you?"...Laughing Joe answered, "Yep a little."

"Been waiting to give it to somebody that will keep my secret. Can you trust your pards'?"

"Yes, they are kin folks." "Well here it is, an good luck." He got up untied Nellie, without another word, wondered off down the road. Joe stood transfixed, watching him go, wondering, "Have I been dreaming? Could this tale he told me be true?" Looking at the crude map in his hand, shaking his head, Joe walked back to the store, bought two cans of peaches, added them to the burro's pack, and headed home.

Stella met him on the porch asking, "Does it take you all day to buy a few groceries?"

"You just come on in the house, and don't think about calling the man with the white jacket, when I tell you'll a fairy tale." Frowning, she followed him in, wondering if he'd been drinking. Joe gathered them all around, and related the story, word for word saying, "And I didn't even get his name."

Steve said, "I know him. He's a legend around here. Calls himself Mountain Jack Finley."

"Do you think there's anything to this map he gave me?"

"I'll bet you my share of the gold...if we find any.....it's just like he said it was. We'll find out." Juanita laughing retorted, "Going off on a dubious trip, following a fairytale and a map on a paper sack! Forget my rocking chair, I'm really staying home now! Just don't tell them old burro's what you're doing." They all had a good laugh.

The next day, telling Juanita good by, and her admonition to them to be careful, they set off on foot, Joe, Eagle and Russ taking turns leading the sometimes balky burros. After a days hike they made their first camp at the pile of rocks, shown on Jack's map, to be the entrance of the hidden trail, near the foot of the mountain.

The next days travel became harder, and more treacherous. Reaching the drop off, it took some doing to lower the loaded burros to the bottom. Steve had slid down first to untie the burros as they came down. The boys and girls held hands, slid down two at a time. Jumped up laughing, "Makes you feel like a kid again," Giggled Stella The traveling grew easier after that, and was enhanced by the beauty it rendered. Deer, elk, even a bear were seen, but paid no attention to the trespassers in their domain.

Steve had lost some of his vigor over the years, but being out in the wilds again seemed to spur him on. The others were young, and strong, took the hardship in stride. Just before the sun set with a golden glow behind the snow capped mountain, ...they wouldn't come near that high....they emerged into what had to be the spot shown on Jack's map.

They unpacked the burros, fixed them something to eat. After they had eaten, they all rolled up in their buffalo robes for a welcome nights sleep.

The morning found them up, ready to start work. While the girls fixed breakfast, Steve and the boys made a survey for suitable timber to build a small cabin with. Steve marking the ones he wanted with a blaze mark.

After breakfast, Steve gave the girls a tin pan each, led them to slow moving, shallow place, demonstrated the way to dip their pan, shake it around, and pick out any small grains of gold....if they found any.... He, and the boys took axes, and saw, began cutting the trees. When they had a good number on the ground, they got the burros, and snaked them to the site. They built two moveable A-frames they could move place to place, to help raise the logs in place.

After a month of backbreaking, sawing, chopping, mud daubing, they were able to stand back, and admire their future home....Laughing Anita joked, "Grandmothers rocking chair would fit right in.".....She had said she wanted no part of this foolishness..

The next chore was to build a sluice box to wash the rock in. Steve was a real wizard with the ax and awl. They cut two pine trees about eight inches in diameter, ten feet long. When finished, they would be the bottom. Steve begun with his short handle ax, that he had the blacksmith hone to a razor sharp edge, slicing one side to a flat surface. Cut groves across it to hold the baffles. Then he groved one side to hold a side board. By the time he had finished the first one, and explaining to Russ, Joe, and Eagle just what, and how he was doing it, they were able to jump right in and help. When the pieces were assembled they scraped resin from some large pines ...they had skinned for that purpose... to use as a seal along the joints, making them practically water tight. Next they built a water tight meat storing box. Sunk it in the ice cold water. Now all their fresh killed meat could be kept on "ice."

They had built a short...in height...frame to build their trough on. Now all they had to do was to trench the stream to flow through the box, and they were in business.

The work had exausted their supplies. Eagle and Joe were elected to take the burros back for more. They would be gone about two or three days. At the steep drop off, they stopped, while Eagle scouted for a way around..... They didn't want to scale that slippery cliff every time they had to go for supplies.....

. Steve kept the girls panning.....they were having some success....while he began the first digging they had attempted.

The first batch of rock he and the girls ran through the sluice box, Stella and Anita were able to harvest enough dust from the bottom of the baffles to cause a little excitement. Giggling Stella queried, "Anita, what are you going to do with all your new found riches?"

"Why Stella, I'm going to have me a resplendent black, and gold coach, two white horses to pull it, with me all dressed up in the finest clothes money can buy."

"Just where are you going in this stupendous getup of yours?"

"Well I'm not sure," she mused with a twinkle in her eye. "What are you going to do with yours?"

"Well, I'm certainly not buying a horse and buggy," she quipped

Steve listening to their banter laughing, not wanting to curb their enthusiasm, needled them saying, "That's hardly enough to buy you girls a pretty dress."

"Well, you'd better start digging, we're going to leave here wealthy women." As they gathered the dust, it was spread out to dry, then bagged it in small cloth bags Juanita had sewn for them.

Even though they were somewhat isolated, Steve, not wanting to take any chances, made preparations to stow their findings away. At the front of the outside fire place, he excavated a fairly deep hole. Lined it with small flat rocks. He searched until he found a large flat rock, fashioned it to fit snugly over the hole. He then did a little landscaping, placed various odds and ends on the top. When he finished he had a undefined vault. Their findings would be placed in there, until they could be transported safely to the bank.

CHAPTER 28

Joe and Eagle returned with a new batch of food, to find Steve and the girls busy washing rock. They happily showed them the results of their work since they had been gone. Joe hugging Stella said, "Well sweetheart, all you need is a big chaw of tobacco, and you'd be a regular prospector."....Which brought him a punch in the belly...

They began work in earnest. The three men digging, the girls panning, and washing rock. Their take growing little by little.

One night they were awakened by a large rumble. Rushing outside to see what had happened, holding a lighted lantern, they could see what had happened. Their digging had undermined a section of rock causing a minor slide. Satisfied, they returned to bed.

The next morning, while breakfast was being prepared, Joe went out to inspect what the slide had done. He returned, holding a hand full of gleaming yellow rocks calling excitedly, "We're rich! we're rich! look at this!." Steve examining them said, "These are not just rocks, but pure gold nuggets! That slide has uncovered a mother lode!" Excited, without waiting for breakfast, they all rushed out to see, and gather the loose nuggets.

They quit the sluice box for now, continued hunting for nuggets. They shoveled dirt and rocks into the pans, searched through the debris salvaging every grain of dust they could. After three week, they decided they had cleaned the area pretty good. They would have to dig some more. But it was time for more supplies. Steve said, "Let's bag what we have up, I'll go for supplies and bank it. You boys can start digging, but be real careful. You saw what could happen, and you might get completely covered up. Have the girls stand back away, and watch for any movement of any kind. A small rock sliding down could be a signal something is going to happen. Eagle reminded him to look for the detour around the steep drop he had marked with blaze marks on trees.

CHAPTER 29

Elkton California

Steve made the trip in fine. Stopping at home, greeting Juanita assuring her the others were just fine, enjoying prospecting. He had brought in the bag with the gold in it, showed it to her. She cried, "Surely you're not going back fore more, ain't that enough for everybody?"

"My dear, there is possibly millions dollars worth in that lode we found. Why go off and leave it for someone else? When we feel we have retrieved all that can reasonably be gotten we will pull out. Those things has the tendency to dry up after a short time." He retrieved a saddle bag from the livery stable, placed the bags of gold evenly in each side, put it across his shoulder, walked nonchalantly over to the bank. Inside he asked to see Mr. Drysdale, the president. He was led back to his office, introduced himself. "Yes sir, what can I do for you today?" Steve opened the saddle bag, laid the contents on his desk. He looked at the sacks a moment, with a dour expression on his face asked, "What's this mean? What's in them dirty sacks you've dumped on my desk?" Steve opened one, poured the gleaming gold nuggets out. Drysdale sat down, reached over, picked one up, eyed it and queried, "Is this real gold?"

"You can bet your bank it is." Drysdale asked, "All them little sacks have gold like this in them?"

"Open them if you like. They contain gold in various sizes. From dust to nuggets."

"You want to store it in my bank."

"Not store, deposit it, with a written receipt signed by you declaring it's exact value. Can you do that and keep it quite? Or must I go somewhere else?"

"Oh yes, we'll be glad to handle that for you. Just a minute, I'll go get a bank officer, to bring his scales."

"Can you trust him to keep it quite also?"

"Yes indeed." He returned with a tall, slim, baldheaded man wearing thick glasses. He proceeded to empty each bag, shake it good, so as not to leave a grain in it. Thirty minutes later he was finished. He looked at Steve, then Mr. Drysdale before saying, "This is fantastic, there is one hundred thousand dollars worth here, at the latest price bulletin I received."

"Fine, write Mr. Steve Alverez a receipt for me to sign."

"Do you think you'll have any more to deposit Mr. Alverez?"

"Well you know this prospecting business depends on luck. I don't know how long mine will hold out." Extending his hand, Drysdale said, "Thank you for using our bank, and may your luck hold true."

Steve spent the rest of the day buying supplies, getting them loaded on the burros. Put them back in the livery stable. He was going to spend the night at home.

On The Trail To Bald Mountain

Steve set off early the next morning. After walking about an hour, he slowed his pace down....which pleased the burros......his years in the wild had attuned his senses. He just had a feeling he was being followed. He walked on, stopping to eat a sandwich from the ones Juanita had prepared for him. About a mile from his turn off, two horsemen passed him, giving a wave but kept going. He went on a little further, stopped, waited for dark. Acted as if he was preparing to camp for the night. The two riders cam back by, again giving him a wave. It being near dark, he didn't think they would be back tonight. He upped his pace to his turn off point, which was the pile of rocks, easily missed in the dark. He turned in, went a hundred yards stopped, tethered one burro in the bushes behind a big tree. He led the other one back to the road, turned, went on up a good half mile. Found a rocky path leading to the right. He went in away, stopped, cut a big leafy branch, spent a good half hour brushing out his entry tracks. He then returned back towards the entrance, working his way below the road. He exited opposite the entrance, went in to where other burro was, tethered the second one. Walked back, again cut a branch, spent an hour brushing out tracks. Saying to himself, "That won't fool an expert tracker, but maybe it'll give me time to make camp and get ready." Night made the treacherous trail more so, but he pushed on, making the camp as breakfast was getting ready.

They all were surprised to see him coming in at that time of day. Anita expressed her concern by asking, "Grandfather surely you didn't come down that awful trail in the night, leading two balky burros!?"

"Well sweetheart, the stork didn't bring me." they had a good laugh to ease the tension.

Steve said, "Let me tell you what happened at the bank first.....that is the good news....and then I'll tell you the bad. Well, I took that bag full of gold in, dumped it on the bank presidents desk. First he wanted to bite my head off for dirtying up his desk. Then he about fainted when I poured out a bag full of the gold on his desk."

"After that it was "Yes sir!" this and "Yes sir!" that. He called in a bank officer with his scales. He was a little bugeyed as he weight it.... They were now leaning forward for the next sentence.... his tally came....he halted a moment, looking at the anxiety on their faces....one hundred thousand dollars worth." They were ecstatic! Sailing on a cloud of euphoria! "Is it true, or are you pulling our leg?" Steve reached in his pocket, withdrew the receipt Drysdale had given him. Gave it to them saying, "Maybe this will help make an honest man out of me." Euphoria reigned again.

Joe, looking at that receipt, had a glorifying image pass through his mind. There was a fortune to made here. A beautiful wife....even in that mining garb she had on... and a full life yet before them. What would the future bring?" Steve let them enjoy the moment for a while. Then he held up his hand, "Now for the bad news. The reason for my time of arrival was the fact I was playing cat and mouse with at least two hombre's tracking me. We have nothing for them to steal at present. My fear is, they might lay back there and ambush us, to take over the claim."

"So beginning after breakfast, two of us men will conceal ourselves out beyond the camp in each direction, with both gun belts, and rifles. If any one is spotted coming our way, fire a warning shot close to him. If he don't retreat, he don't come any further, if you know what I mean. We'll be protecting our lives, and the claim. The third man will rotate with one of us every two hours. The girls will remain inside, until we find out what is coming off, agreed?" A course of 'yes' ended the speech.

CHAPTER 30

At the Gold Mine: Bald Mountain

They kept up the vigil for two days and nights, but nothing happened. Steve, believing he had been wrong, called it off. But he tethered the burros up the trail a piece where he could watch them. They would recognize trouble before anyone else.

They went back to work. The men excavating, the girls working the sluice box. It wasn't until two days later that they discovered their safety was still in jeopardy.

Anita, and Stella, were working at the sluice box, when a rifle shot reverberated through the mountain. A bullet buried it's self in the side of the box right beside Stella. Both girls screamed, and ran for the protection of the cabin. Joe seen and heard what happened. He looked up the hill, made a judgment where the shot had came from, grabbed his rifle, jumped across the stream, made a wide circle, hoping to come in behind the culprit. When he thought he was high enough, he changed his route. Walking very slow, and quietly as possible. He eased on around, eyes searching for any sign of the shooter. Suddenly he halted in his tracks, sniffed the air, smelled tobacco smoke. A few quiet steps brought him to a point he could see a black sombrero. A few more short easy steps, his sensitive feet feeling for any stick or twig that would snap and give him away. He stopped short, right behind the man, who was still smoking, and peering down toward the camp. He pulled the hammer back on his gun, making a very identifying noise. His adversary leaped up, turned to face him, making no attempt to raise his rifle. He knew to do so, would bring a hot bullet from Joe's gun, right through his chest. Joe asked, "Just what are you doing up here? That shot you fired almost killed my wife?"

"I'm up here on orders from my boss, to run you people out of your diggings down there."

"Who is your boss?" He started to reach in his pocket. Joe raised his gun menacingly, "Careful now, what's in there?"

"Just let me get it, and I'll show you."

"Go on, but no quick moves." He came out with a slip of paper, handed it to Joe. "Ok, now slowly lay that gun on the ground, and back up a step or two." When he had done as he was told, still keeping a wary eye on him, Joe read it. First noticing it was written on the bank of Elkton paper. It read, "Follow that man Alverez. See where he goes. He has struck a mother lode, a gold mine." Drysdale.

"He give you this paper himself?"

"Yep, called me in his office, writ it, and told me what he wanted done"

"What else do you do for him?"

"Just guard the bank at night."

"How many more men work for him in this manner?"

"None as I know of."

"What is your name?"

"Woodrow Epling."

"Well Woody, suppose you start walking down to the camp. My friends would like to meet you. They might even have a new rope you'd like to see."

"You mean hang me?"

"Yep, that's what new ropes are for."

"Now look here, I didn't hurt anybody."

"No, but you tried. And if I hadn't caught you would have. Start walking." In camp, they all gathered around for a look at the hombre Joe had brought in. Stella had gone from being frightened to being mad. She took a look at him, started fingering her gun. Joe caught her eye, shook his head no. she turned and stamped away. Joe handed Steve the slip of paper. He read it, looked at Epling with eyes spouting fire, "Just how did you find this place?"

"I walked along the road, following the burro tracks. Suddenly there was only one. There was a faint trail leading off to the left. I followed it, until I found two tracks again."

"Well, I did say my cat and mouse trick wouldn't fool an expert tracker, didn't I?" Steve quoted. "How did you learn to track that well?"

"I was a tracker and scout for the army up there at Fort Kilgore. Until I got in a fight with two Indian scouts, and the Colonel kicked me out." "Well, I don't allow they'll kick you out of where you're going now."

"We'll take a trip into Elkton tomorrow. I'll introduce you to the sheriff, then make a call on Mr. Drysdale."

"I'm afraid you won't catch him there."

"Why not?"

"He was leaving for Sacramento the day I left."

"Oh, he had business there?"

"Yep, he was taking a strong box with him. Something for the big bank there." Steve gave the others a incredulous look, and they were quick to decipher what it meant. Their hard earned gold was disappearing.

"I want Eagle to go along with me. I might need some help." The others gave him an inquiring look. "I don't mean with him, I'm talking about when I get in town. My intuition tells me more is going on than we expect." Turning to Woody he asked, "Does many men, not towns people, drift in pretty regular to see Drysdale?"

"There's three or four that come in. Always go to his office."

"Would you say they're business men?"

"Naw, not dressed like they are."

"How is that?"

"Like cowboys, with dusty clothes, like they had ridden a ways."

"Was your orders from Drysdale to kill us?"

"He didn't say kill, he said run 'em off. I wouldn't think about killing anybody. I didn't shoot at the girls to hit 'em, just to scare them enough that they would want you men to take them away. I wasn't wait'n to shoot any more, but to see if you'll would hightail it, when this man...nodding to Joe...slipped up on me."

"Has he ever asked you to do anything like this before?"

"Just to follow a man, see where he went, and who he talked to, not to bother him."

"Was he a business man?"

"Naw, a miner."

"Could you identify these people you have told us about?"

"Yep, I'd know 'em if I see 'em again."

"Ok, you sit there for a minute."

Steve motioned the others over out of hearing. "Look, we have a lot at stake. I don't think this guy is bad, I believe he has been coerced into doing these things. I want to trust him, believing he might be of some help to us in finding our gold. I'm sure it never reached Sacramento. What is your opinion?"

"I agree, he didn't appear like an outlaw to me, when I cornered him up on the hill."

"Stella, what's your opinion? Do you believe he shot just to scare you girls, like he said?"

"Well, studying him closely, watching his reactions to your questions, I believe you're right."

CHAPTER 31

The Man Hunt

Leaving the others to continue working, with a warning to keep a watchful eye, Steve and Eagle, with Woody in tow, left for Elkton.

After checking in on Juanita, they moseyed around town, giving Woody a chance

to see if there was anyone around he could recognize. Seeing no one, they went to the bank. Steve presented his receipt at the teller's window, "I'd like withdraw this please." The teller scrutinized him, "I'll be back in a moment." He returned with the bank officer who had weighed the gold, and wrote the receipt for Drysdale to sign. "Good day Mr. Alverez, I'm afraid I can't return your deposit. Mr. Drysdale took it, and some more deposits to Sacramento to the Federal Bank there. He became concerned about all the robberies around here, thought they would be much safer there.."

"Ok, thank you."

They left went to the stage coach office, bought tickets to Sacramento on the stage leaving at noon. They wondered around looking, until it was time to catch the stage.

Arriving there too late to go to the bank, they obtained rooms at the hotel. The next morning they asked directions to the bank. Finding it, they entered, went to the teller's window. Steve presented his receipt. The teller said, "I don't believe you have an account here. When was it deposited?"

"I didn't deposit it personally. Mr. Drysdale from the bank in Elkton, was supposed to deposit it for me."

"I'm sorry Sir, there have been no such deposit made. Mr. Drysdale hasn't been to this bank in quite sometime." Crestfallen, but knowing full well it was just as he expected, they left. Outside they pondered their next move. They decided to wait until the next stage coach came in, make inquires from the driver, to see if he remembered carrying a man, and a strong box here.

When the stage coach arrived, they waited until the driver wasn't busy, approached him asking, "Do you remember bringing a gentleman with a strong box here a few days ago?" The driver, a heavy set, tobacco chewing man, looked at them quizzically, "Are you the law of some kind?"

"No, just interested in finding a friend."

"Yep, I remember him, but he didn't come all the way here. Asked me to let him off at Mosley. There was a buggy and driver waiting for him. I handed down the box, he loaded it in the buggy, and they drove away to the west. Does that help you any?"

"Yes, just fine, extending his hand, thank you."

"Well Eagle, as the little boy said, whew! I smell a skonk'. Are you good at tracking "skonks'?"

"I've never been interested in tracking the four legged kind, but the two legged ones are a different thing. I can smell 'em a mile away."

"Well, here we are, no horses. I hope the livery stable has a three to rent us. Let's find out." They rented horses, and set out for Mosley.

Arriving there, they asked a hombre, standing in front of the saloon, "Would you happen to know a nan named Drysdale around these parts?"

"Well, I think there is a man by that name, owns a ranch with his partners, up north of here."

"Thanks."

They started off in that direction. "He didn't say how far," quoted Eagle. Laughing, Steve said, "Ok scout, let's start scouting."

It wasn't long before they began to see cattle grazing off to their left. They altered course a bit, and soon saw in the distance, a ranch house, set back in a grove of trees. They moved forward, stopping on a knoll where they could observe the house, and surroundings. They moved back into the trees far enough not to be seen. Eagle asked, "What is your plan?"

"We'll stay here watching to see how much activity goes on down there, try to find out how many men are there. After dark, we'll walk our horses up close, leave them hidden in the trees, sneak up to a window, and see who might be in there. If things look right, we'll simply bust in, and confront who ever is there, and play it from there. What do you suggest?"

"Let Woody and me see if there is a back door, see if we can slip in that way. You watch from your window until we can get things under control, and let you in. That way we won't create so much noise. I see, what is probably a bunk house. There might be more than we can take on."

"You're right. Maybe we can get what we want, slip out the back way."

After dark, when things had settled down, they eased on up to the house, checking to see if there was a back door. There was, and it was dark inside. Leaving them there, Steve went back around to a window looking into the living room. Peeking in, he could see two people. One of them was Drysdale!

As he watched, he saw Eagle and Woody enter the room, guns drawn. He wasn't able to hear any conversation, but was able to see the two jump up, facing Eagle and Woody. In a moment Woody moved toward the door, he went on around, and entered. Dryadale was saying, "Woodrow, as much as I was paying you, did you have to turn traitor?" Laughing Woody said, "I'll give you your money back. That is, if you live long enough to use it." Drysdale said, "You know all I have to do is give a yell to alert my men out in the bunk house."

"One word, and you and your partner there will, as Woody said, not live long enough to spend his money." Woody walked up behind Drysdale, put the barrel of his gun in his back. Steve facing him said, "Looks like I put my trust in a bad place. So you're going to take us to that box you brought here with you. Let's move." No movement. Steve said again, "NOW!" Drysdale drew a deep breath, let out a yell you could have heard a mile away. Woody pulled the trigger on his gun, Drysdale fell to the floor dead. His partner raised his hands.

Eagle and Woody ran to the door, and out on the porch, just as four men emerged from the bunk house. Eagle fired a shot in the dirt at their feet, called to them, "Your boss is dead. If you want to join him, keep coming." They stopped in their tracks. One of them called back, "Don't know who you are Mr. But we ain't got no quarrel with you. Is Mr. Douglas in there?"

"Yes, stay there, he'll be out in a minute."

In the house, Steve asked the partner, "Do you know about the box I was talking about?"

"Yes, I know there was a box. There is one up stairs, maybe that's the one you want."

"Ok, lead on, show me." Sure enough, the strong box was there. Steve knocked the lock off with the butt of his gun, opened it to reveal the small bags stacked in rows. He picked up one, opened it, to make sure. It was gold all right. He retied the bag, placed it back in the box, "Did you know what was in here?"

"Well, I thought it must be money, I wasn't sure about gold. He told me that he was planning to go East, start a business."

"Did he offer you a partnership in that enterprise?"

"No, I was to stay here, run the ranch, like I have been."

"Did you know he was stealing it?"

"I had an idea he was running off with bank money."

"Help me down the stairs with this, ok?"

"Sure"

Down stairs, Eagle asked him, "Your name Douglas?"

"Yes"

"Your men out there want to see you." He walked out on the porch, called to the men, "Mr. Drysdale is dead of his own doing. The ranch will continue to operate as before. If some of you will come in carry his body out. We'll burry him in the morning."

Woody went over, led their horses to the house. When they were ready to leave, Steve said, "Mr. Douglas, we're sorry this had to happen, but I think you understand." Extending his hand said, "Thank you for your cooperation, and good luck."

"Same to you'll."

They left, on their way back to Sacramento, taking turns holding the box in the saddle with them.

On the way they decided it best to leave their money in the bank in Sacramento. They returned the horses to the livery stable, took the strong box to the bank, which was more than happy to make them a joint account. They listed the names, adding Woody's name to the list. They were given a receipt. As they left, Woody asked, "Why did you add my name? I have done none of the work to earn it."

"Oh yes you have. And if it's work you're interested in, there is plenty left when we get back," Steve assured him.

CHAPTER 32

At the Camp on Bald Mountain

They caught the stage back to Elkton. Spent the night at his house, telling Juanita about all that happened in Sacramento, and promising her he would send the girls home for a rest. The next morning they left for the camp.

Every one at the camp was elated to see them, and hungry for the news of what had transpired..

Joe, Russ and the girls had done a masterful job of mining. They hadaccumulated as much, if not more, than they hauled away. Had it well hidden in Steve's vault, and had no more interference.

They had made out well with their supplies. Joe had killed a deer, so they had fresh meat. Their only problem had been, both girls had been complaining of being sick, especially in the morning. Steve knowingly, chose that time to tell them they were going in with the supply trip tomorrow. They protested, but it fell on deft ears.

Joe and Russ both were elected to take the burros, and the girls in. Bring back more supplies. Steve and Woody would continue to work the mine while they were gone.

The next morning they were ready to depart. Anita and Stella, acting bravely, but were stifling tears as they bid goodby.

Jaunita was overjoyed to see the girls. After embracing them, she stood back looking them over good saying, "My but you look so strong and healthy, the hard work was outwardly good for you, but I know you will be happy to have a good bath, and rest for a while." She embraced Russ and Joe too, "When are you going back?"

"Just as soon as we get the supplies."

"Does it have to be so soon?"

"Yes, we're anxious to harvest all we can before something else happens."

The next morning, with the burro's loaded, they kissed their wives, and Juanita goodby, reassuring them they would be careful, and return as often as possible, and left for the camp on Bald Mountain.

On their arrival at camp, they pitched right in with Steve and Woody operating the mine. Taking turns digging, and working at the sluice trough.

At the end of four months, leaving only for more supplies, they discovered the amount of nuggets, and dust dwindling. It ended just as it started, suddenly. One day there was a little dust to be found the next day nothing. Steve standing back looking at the dent they had made in the rock, shook his head asserted, "That the way these thing go. First there is a vein, seemly without end, then nothing. Thanks to old Mountain Jack, we have done quite well for ourselves. The assayer will tell us how much."

CHAPTER 33

On his last trip in, Steve had brought back material to build two boxes, figuring the lode was about to run out.

They got busy, made two of a size two men could carry between them. The small bags were packed in, the top set in place, with a hasp and lock.

They checked around the camp. Gathered up all the tools, placed them in the cabin. Satisfied everything was taken care of, they had a good nights rest.

The next morning, they loaded one box on each burro, covered them with buffalo robes. When they ready to leave Steve said, "Joe, you and Russ set fire to the cabin, Woody and I'll destroy the sluice trough. We want to leave the impression we had hit a dry hole. It just might be possible we want to return, and try further around the mountain." ....Drawing looks of scepticism from the others....

They discussed their next move. Steve suggested, "They wait at the road, flag down the stage coach on it's way to Sacramento. He, Joe, Russ and Eagle would take the boxes to the bank there. Woody could take the burros to Elkton."

"When the gold was assayed, the total, plus the hundred thousand already there would be divided four ways." He stopped to ask Woody if he wanted to leave his portion there in that bank, as he proposed to do with his. "Yes, that would suit me fine. I don't trust the bank in Elkton, since what happened to you." He continued, "Joe Russ, and Eagle can decide what they want to do while we're there at the bank. Then we'll return to Elkton. Is this agreeable with everyone?" Affirmative answers settled it.

As they were about to set fire to the cabin, the burro's began making a noise, their ears perked up, an indication someone was coming. In a few minutes, the intruder appeared. To their surprise, it was Mountain Jack and Nellie. "Howdy folks, looks like you're leaving. No luck uh?" Joe spoke up, "Oh yes, we really did well. I've been wondering how to find you, to give your part. It was your advice that made it happen. If you wait just a minute, we'll give your share."

"No! No! Don't want it, have no use for it. Some rogue would probably kill me for it."

"Well wait a minute anyway." He went to one of the burros, came back carrying the two cans of peaches he had bought just in case he ever saw him again. Grinning broadly, he took the cans, looked at them fondly saying, "Beats gold 'eny old day. Thank you. You ain't going to burn the cabin down are you?"

"Yes, that's just what we're getting ready to do."

"Would you'll mind saving it for me? Cum in mighty handy when the cold wind starts blowing up har."

"Sure we'll save it for you. Hope it brings you as much good luck as it did us."

"Well thank ye again." With that he went on down the trail humming to himself.

Satisfied everything had been taken care of, with a fond last look, they departed.

CHAPTER 34

The Bank In Sacramento

When the stage entered Sacramento, Steve riding on top with the driver asked, "Would you mind stopping in front of the bank for us?" The driver, emitting a stream of tobacco juice over the side said, "Yep, be glad to."

He stopped, the two boxes were handed down. Steve thanked him, and with a wave, cracked his whip over the team's back, he was off.

They toted the boxes in, and was directed to a room where it was assayed. The assayer was amazed at the total of one million five hundred thousand dollars worth.

Shaking his head asked, "You have done well, where did you find such a strike." Steve Laughing, with tongue in cheek said, "Oh it was easy, found it in a bunch of burro tracks." The man looked at him strangely for a moment, then realizing he was joking, laughed, They must have been mighty deep tracks."

"How do you want this taken care of?"

"We want the one hundred thousand dollars that was deposited before, added to this you have counted today, and divide it into four equal parts. I want my part to stay here in this bank. The same for Woodrow Epling. A receipt and account book for Steve Alverez, and Woodrow Epling made out and given to me now. These two gentlemen can tell you what to do with theirs." Joe said, "I want a thousand dollars cash, and a bank check for the rest so I can deposit it in my home town bank."

"Your name is?"

"Joe Wiseman." He wrote that down, turned to look at Russ. "And how Do want your's handled?"

"The same way Joe here did. My name is Russ Wiseman."

"Brothers huh?"

"No sir, cousins." Eagle came next. "Mine fixed the same as these the two, nodding to Joe and Russ. My name is Eagle."

"Eagle what?" He glanced at Joe, who by instinct, knew what he was thinking, gave a nod of his head. He answered, "Eagle Wiseman."

"Another cousin?" "No, brothers." Added Joe.

He looked skeptical, but said nothing. "Ok gentlemen, if you'll have a seat, I'll get the paper work done, and get back with you."

While they waited, Eagle said to Joe, "I don't know what to say about you saying brothers, although I've felt like that." Joe stood, put his arm's around

him, feeling a lump in his throat said. "As far as I'm concerned, and so does Mom and Dad, forvc that matter, consider you my brother." Giving him a light punch on the arm, "I wouldn't trade you for any amount of "real" brothers."....
The pride showing brightly in Eagle's eyes....

The man returned with his paper work. Handed Steve his and Woody's pass book and deposit receipt, showing a deposit of four hundred thousand dollars. Handed Joe, Eagle and Russ their cash in an envelope, and a Cashiers check for three hundred ninety nine thousand dollars. The transaction completed, he extended his hand, to shake hand's with each one saying, "Gentlemen thank you for trusting your hard earned money to our bank, and we'll be happy to serve more at any time." They thanked him, and departed. They had finished in time to catch the next stage coach to Elkton.

CHAPTER 35

Elkton California
1848

The women were overjoyed to see their men again. After all the embracing was done, Steve handed his pass book to Juanita declaring, "Well Mrs. Alverez, it looks like you married the right man. She opened the pass book, looked up astounded! "Well Mr. Alverez, this is nice, but I've long ago, known I had married the right man ." Stella, with her arms still around Joe's neck, smiling said, "Just one look at this handsome man, even when he was unconscious, I knew he was the only man for me." Joe kissed her sweetly, "Now ain't that just like a woman, take advantage of a man while he's asleep?" He pushed her back a little, looking at her belly asked, "Why didn't you tell me about this before you left camp?"

"Didn't want you worrying about me. Anita did the same thing." Looking at Anita Joe said, "Russ you have a conspirator too ."

"So I have noticed."

"Well ain't you both going to say you're happy, or just stand there looking?" They both took their wife in their arm's again saying, "Of course we're happy, and would have said so, if you'd given us time." Steve chided. "Now let's not have a acrimonious family dispute. We're all equally ecstatic." They all laughed, and things moved back to blissful peace.

They rested a week, before retrieving their covered wagon, and going to their separate homes. Woody had already left, going home to see his parents. Juanita was worried about the girls traveling in the wagon in their condition. They had kept the buffalo robes from their mining expedition. They were added to the bedding in it, hoping that would make it more comfortable.

The road home

With much tearful embracing, the one wagon 'wagon train' left ElktonCalifornia for Gila Springs, Sundown, and Youngstown Arizona.

They traveled at a slow pace, to make it easy on Anita and Stella, camping over night twice, before reaching Ed and Helen's ranch, a short distance out of Gila Springs. There was more happy embracing from Ed, Helen, and Mggie,

Eagle's mother, They spent the night telling them of their adventure gold mining. They each showed them their pass book, and check. They were positively astounded at the amount, but gloriously happy they had made it safely back home.

Their most joyful news was, to learn they were going to grandparents. They were extremely happy for Anita and Russ also.

The next morning found Russ, and Anita on their way to Sundown. Their home with Ben, and Jenny. Eagle had made his case with his mother, and was going with them. He was to stay with Joe and Stella...they had secretly agreed to it....

Ben and Jenny was delight to see them, and hear all about their gold mining experience. Found it hard to believe the amount of money they had earned, until Russ showed them his pass book, and check. Flabbergasted when they read the figures.

As with Ed and Helen, they were ecstatic to learn they were going to be grandparents. They were blithesomely happy for Stella and Joe also.

After a good nights rest...in a bed...Joe and Stella were ready for the last leg of their journey.

Reaching home, Joe stored the wagon by the barn, turned the horses out to pasture....they had earned a good rest....

The next day he and Eagle went to the bank and deposited their checks. While there, they noticed a sign on the bulletin board stating the Claybern ranch was up for sale. Asking the teller about it. He said, "Yes, the bank foreclosed on it." They asked the price, was given a figure. When they returned home, talked it over with Stella. Joe, and Eagle decided to buy it as partner's. They went to the bank, completed the transaction, and became the new owner's. Since the two ranches joined each other, they named it the 'Bar-W-W.'...Bar Wiseman Wiseman... One of the largest ranches in the Arizona Territory.

CHAPTER 36

The Bar- W-W Ranch June
1849

On June the 12th a fine healthy boy was born to Stella and Joe He was named Edwin Albert after both their fathers....they were to learn that two days later, Anita and Russ were the proud parents of a fine boy also. Named Steven Ben. Steven after her grandfather, Ben after Russ's father.....

The moon must have been right, Two days later, Joe's horse Kicker, and Stella's mare Millie were the parents of a frisky colt, Kicker 11.

Over on the newly acquired ranch, Eagle was quick to take the reins. He weeded out the Claybern hands...he didn't need slouchy gun-slingers. He wanted, and hired, honest hard-working cowboys.

After he had things running the way he wanted, he stopped by one day, to tell Joe he would be gone a few days, and asked if he would he look in on his people until he returned . Joe being so close to him, knew by instinct what he was up to. Grinning he said, "Sure thing partner, have a good trip."

A week later, Eagle returned driving a handsome buggy, ...with his horse trailing behind.... In the seat beside him was a lovely Navaho Indian girl. Joe and Stella went out to meet them. Eagle jumped down, reached up lifted her down, put his arm's around her waist, smiling broadly said, "Joe and Stella Wisemam, please welcome my wife, Mrs. Rose Eagle Wiseman." While Joe shook hand's and pounded Eagle on the back, Stella went to Rose, embraced her saying, "Welcome to the family. How in the world did that big guy fool a pretty girl like you?"

"Oh, he didn't do the fooling, I did. We were children together. At that young age, I kept telling myself I'm going to have him as,...wee-CHAH-kh-chah,..my true husband." Stella then embraced Eagle saying, "You're a very lucky man, I'm so happy for you both."

Word was sent to Ed, Helen, and Maggie, as well as Russ and Anita, about the happy event, along with a date, on which there was going to be a big party for them, and they must attend.

On the appointed time, every one was there. A barbecue was made ready, as well as some Indian food Rose and Maggie made. Joe found in his crew, a guitar playing cowboy. They had a wonderful week of revelry. Anita, ...an to everyone's surprise ...Rose, with a beautiful voice, accompanied by the guitar, sang beautiful songs, while the others danced. Eagle, proud as a peacock, strutted about, accepting congratulations. Maggie too was extremely proud of her son.

It was over all too soon. The guests departed for home.

CHAPTER 37

The Civil War Years
The West Territories
1861-1865
A Bit of History

The area known as The New Mexico Territory, comprised of a portion of Nevada, and California, was ceded to the United States in 1848, after the Mexican War. The Southern portion, The Arizona Territory was purchased from Mexico in 1854, but still included as part of the New Mexico Territory.

The leaders in the Arizona territory, appealed to the Federal government for separate recognition as a Territory, but the request was ignored.

When the disputes in the East erupted into Civil war, a Confederate Congress, in March 1861, declared the secession of the Arizona from the New Mexico Territory, creating the West's only Confederate Territory.

This began a shift of Union troops to the east, leaving a thin number scattered in vacated Forts, along the Rio Grand, to await the expected Confederate invasion. Also a number of Union Officers resigned their commissions, going over to the Confederate South.

One such Officer was Major Henry H. Sibley. He traveled to Richmond, trying to convince the Confederate leaders of the vast opportunities that existed in the West. This caught the attention of Jefferson Davis. He Commissioned Sibley as a Brigadier General. Sent him to Texas, to raise an army of the Confederacy, to ..,/ expand it's interest in that area. Especially the control of the New Mexico Territory, linking it, with California, and the Pacific Ocean the far West. A possible way to beat the Union blockade in the Atlantic.

CHAPTER 38

The Bar-W-W Ranch
1862

The Wiseman Ranches having herds of beef ready for the market, were in a quandary as what to do. Thinking it too dangerous to try for the Santa Fe market, they decided to contact a ranching friend in Utah, to see if he could, and would take their cattle, until other arrangements could be made

A deal was made, and a concentrated effort was made to round up the cattle. And horses, move them to a central location, and the drive was begun. They were delivered with only a minor attack by Indians, netting a loss of a few head.

With the stock safe for the time being, it was time to assess their situation in regard to the mounting confusion taking place around them..

It was decided that the three young families band together for better protection. Eagles place being the larger, they would use it. Joe, Stella and their son. Russ Anita, and their son would move there. Ben and Jenney would move to Gila Springs with Ed and Helen.

Since they had rarely visited each other, it would be a great chance for the boys, now twelve years old, to get to know each other, and become fast friends.

After they were all settled in, Joe, Russ and Eagle talked at length, about what course they would take in the conflict. Two incidents, coming close together decided their fate for the rest of the war.

One afternoon, a group of what appeared to be Confederate Cavalry, rode into the yard in front of the house. They remained mounted until Joe, Eagle and Russ, stepped out on the top step of the porch. Then three of them dismounted, walked to the bottom of the steps. One wore the insignia of a Captain, one that of a Lieutenant, the third the chevrons of a Sergeant. The four remaining mounted, were troopers.

The Captain placed one foot on the step, gave a gesture, somewhat resembling a salute. In a voice reeking with arrogant authority stated, "General Garland's Compliments Sir. I am Captain Lamb, this is Lieutenant Weaver, Sergeant Ross, and four troopers from the 4th Arizona Cavalry. We're here to take possession of this residence for his Headquarters when he arrives later this week. He will, on arrival, issue you a certificate on the treasure of C. S. A. For payment of it's use."

By this time, the three women had stepped outside the door, standing transfixed, horrified, at what they were hearing. "The General will require the front room for his office, and sleeping arrangements for himself and his staff. That can be determined later. For now, we will requite one room for the Lieutenant and myself."

"The Sergeant will stay in the bunk house with these troopers. Your men will move to the barn. While we attend to our horses, we expect to take the evening meal, served here on the porch, as soon as possible. Have I made this all perfectly clear?" Joe grunted, "Yes you have. While you tend to your horses, I will see that the bunk house is cleared for your men." He stepped back to Eagle, "Take the women inside, help them throw some kind of a meal together, Send the boys up stairs, warn them to stay there. If these hoodlums are soldiers, I'm an Admiral in the Arizona Navy."

He walked over to the bunk house. The men were standing in the door, straining to see and hear what was going on. He motioned them inside, speaking in a low voice he said, "I want you boys to roll your rifles, and hand guns, in your bed roll, go to the barn, as if you intended to spend the night. But I want that bunk house guarded at all times after dark. There's going to be trouble. They are to be kept out of it.

As they trudged, seemingly disgruntled, at having to move, the troopers, laughing, taunted them, "Nothing like a good roll in the hay, huh cowboy?"

"Better than sleeping with them bed bugs, in that bunk house." Fred McCoy, the foreman, shot back." One of them sneered back, "Ok pop, we'll teach you a few manners before we leave here."

The women set them out a supper of corn bread, beans, and boiled potatoes, which they wolfed down like hogs at the slop trough, drinking from a jug the Captain brought in. Meanwhile Stella asked, "What bed room are we going to put them in?" Joe responded, "They won't be allowed in any room. My guess is, that they'll drink themselves into a stupor, pass out right there on the floor....That didn't happen...

They drank, laughed, at bawdy jokes until almost midnight. The Captain staggered up calling, "Whars them women, why haven't they joined the party?" With that, he wobbled into the living room, looked around, spotting a closed door, staggered his way over, jerked it open. The women were huddled on the bed talking, jumped up at the sound of the door opening, stifling a scream, demanded, "What are you doing in here? Get out now!" He guffawed, "We want to dance, come on out here."

Joe had eased a door open behind him, while Eagle slipped out to the back door, opened it quietly, moved inside, where could watch the two on the porch.

In the bed room, the Captain was saying, "Ah an Indian wench. I always wanted one. Taking a step toward Rose." She flew into him. Ten seconds later, he staggered backward, face and nose bleeding, Barely able to open his scratched eyes. "A wild cat he rasped. Well I like 'em wild." Reaching down to his boot, withdrew a large hunting knife sneering, "This will take a little of that wildness out." Joe, behind him, gun drawn said, "You just drop that knife to the floor now!" Startled, he whirled, raised his arm threw the knife at Joe. It embedded it's self in the door jam, just as he fell to the floor, a bullet hole between his eyes. The remaining two rushed inside, to find Eagle with his gun pointed at them saying, "You boys just stand where you are. Unbuckle them gun belts, lay them on the floor. Then take them frog stickers out of your boots, lay them there too, then step back up two steps."

The four out in the bunk house, hearing the shot, rushed out the door, right into six drawn six-guns. Fred quipped, "Didn't I tell you them bed bugs were hell? Let's drop them gun belts where you stand, then march right over to the porch, see what's going on."

Joe walked out to the living room, looking with disdain on the two there. ordered, "You two go in there, carry your leader out side, saddle his horse, tie him across it." See the other four, being ushered up on the porch, instructed his men, "Search them for knives, the others had them in their boots. Take them out to saddle their horses, and tie their hands. Saddle yours, and our three....indicating himself, Russ and Eagle....we have a long ride by daylight. We're going to deliver these coyotes to the army at Fort Gilmore, show them what outstanding cavalrymen they have."

They arrived at the gate of the Fort an hour after daylight. The sentry called the Sergeant of the Guard, who came in a trot, bringing four men with him. After hearing a partial explanation, the Sergeant hurried to seek the Colonel, who appeared partly dressed. Joe speaking, gave him the whole sordid story.

The Colonel, looking them over, turned with a sigh of disgust, replied angrily, "These men are deserters. They were sent out on patrol the day before yesterday, never returned. And evidently had no intention of ever returning." He turned to the Sergeant of the Guard, "Have them burry the dead one, then lock them up to stand trial for desertion." Bowing his head he added, "Gentlemen, I offer you my, and the Armies, most sincere apology for this damnable deed inflicted upon you and your family. I hope you will understand, that in recruiting men for this terrible conflict we're now facing, there is bound to be some rotten apples in the barrel."

"Yes Sir, I reckon so. Your apology is accepted, the incident is concluded." Shaking hands, they departed for home.

CHAPTER 39

The second incident was quite a bit more pleasant. A rider came rushing into the yard, dropped the reins to his horse, bounded up on the porch, just as Eagle opened the door. The rider nervously pronounced, "Union Officer headed this way."

"By himself?"

"Yes sir"

"Ok son, thank you"

Eagle waited on the porch until the Officer rode into the yard. He couldn't believe his eyes. Who should dismount but a laughing Art McMagee All decked out in a splendid Union uniform, with a Colonel's insignia on his shoulder epaulet.

Eagle bounded of the porch, shook his hand, then embraced him. Art jumped back laughing, "Look here my boy, you don't go around hugging Colonels, it ain't manly." Mischievously Eagle did it again, took him by the arm, "Come on in the house, there's a couple more guys waiting to hug you."

After all the hugging, hand shaking and back slapping, by Russ and Joe Stella, Anita and Rose...she had never met him, but joined in after the introduction...came in to greet him with Hughs. Art, completely taken back by such a greeting asked, "Can I go out and come in again?" After a good laugh, they settled down to talk, while the ladies prepared refreshments.

Eagle said, "What did you do re-enlist? I heard you tell that Colonel one time, they wouldn't let you back in the army."

"Well my old nemesis General Foley was transferred to the East. The new Western Department Commander happened to be an old friend. I served as his Aide, back when he was a Brigadier General. As soon as he took over, he sent for me. Offered me the brevet rank of Colonel, and command of Fort Upshire, and the 5th Cavalry."

"The previous Commander, and most of the troops, had been transferred to the East. It will be my job to reorganize, bring in troops, left scattered in isolated post, all along the Rio Grande. Build a strong force, to block any Confederate invasion from California. Their aim would be to join the Confederates coming up from Texas.

"I guess by now, you are wondering what brought me here, besides a wonderful social visit. What I really want to do, is organize a fast, hard hitting cavalry unit for two goals. One to protect our supply trains on the Santa Fe trail from the Apaches. The other, I already mentioned, to patrol our Western border against the Californians. Fort Upshire, as you probably know, is located over just West of the New Mexico border. The units I mentioned would operate from there, joining other Union forces in Central, and Northen Arizona, when assistance is needed."

Joe interrupted Art, to tell him about the incident with the Confederate deserters, and asked, "What is to be done about situations like that?"

"Well those are isolated cases. You can't guard each individual ranch or farm, you could only help if you happened to be there at the time." Eagle said, "What we have discussed between ourselves, is an independent unit, acting as a police force, guarding against incidents like that, and harassing Confederate outpost, and supply trains, and depots. Does that make any sense to you?"

"Absolutely, that is what I've been trying to explain. Maybe not in the same words."

"Would you three be interested in organizing, and commanding such a unit?"

"We'll give it some thought. But we three must be together, not separated into different units."

"That can be worked out. How about this? I am authorised to give you each the Brevet Rank of Captain, furnish uniforms, arms, and supplies. You recruit your own men, who must take the oath of allegiance to the Union, and be expert horsemen. You can arrange them in any kind of units you want. Spend as time training as possible.. You will be under my command only. Other Commanders may ask you for assistance, but cannot command you to do so."

"What about our families?"

"You have two choices. You can move them into the fort, where they wouldn't be much safer, since Forts are attacked with heavy artillery causing greater damage. Or leave them where they are. I personally believe that best, since you as an independent force will be patrolling much of your time in this area."

Stella entered smiling, "I hate to disturb you Gentlemen, but dinner is on the table, your presence is desired, before it all disappears."

When they came in the dining room, the boys rose from the table. Joe said, "Art, I'd like you to meet three future cavalrymen...drawing an icy look from Stella... Placing his arm around each one, as he introduced them. This is Stella and my son Edwin. This is Steven, Russ and Anita's son. This is Dan, Eagle and Rose's son. They are all twelve years old now. Art shook hands with them, expressing what fine young men they were. "You know it's hard to believe so much time has passed, since I met you folks. Working with you men was one of my greatest experiences. It is my fervent wish, there will be no need for

Cavalrymen, to fight in wars, when these young men are grown." A voice of AMEN echoed through the room!

CHAPTER 40

After dinner, Art announced he had to make a trip down South, rounding up more troops, from those left behind, when their Commander, and most of his troops were dispatched Eastward. He said, "I'll be back the latter part of the week to check on your decision. After you have fully discussed it between yourselves and your family." Thanking the ladies for an excellent meal, shaking hands with the men, and the boys, he departed.

Joe gathered them all in the living room, to analyze, and discuss the situation. The boys realizing this was going to be an important family discussion, quietly found them a seat in the corner to listen.

Stella stood, walked over to stand by Joe. Laid her arm across his shoulder, began the discussion, "There is no use for us to set here haggling over this or that point. We women had our talk, while you men were talking. We understand the importance of the decision you have to make. We will be very proud of, and stand behind you, what ever you decide. Now if you will excuse us, we'll leave you to your discussion." Joe immediately stood, a little bleary eyed, took her in his arms in a tender embrace, that told her of the love in his heart that words could not.

After they all had embraced, Stella led the women out of the room, taking the boys with them. The room remained perfectly quiet for a while. The men sat looking at each other, the love and pride in their hearts, showing in their eyes.

When the discussion started again, it was short, and to the point. Eagle proposed they accept Arts terms, only if he would provide at least thirty qualified men along with the arms, and supplies. The proposal was unanimously accepted. All there was to do now, was wait for Art's return, to get his answer.

Art returned by the end of the week, as he promised. He was greeted warmly, and invited to dinner, while they talked.

Anxious for their decision, he asked right off, "Have you men reached a decision, suitable to everyone?"

"Yes we have, with one stipulation." With raised eyebrows, he said, "You name it, I'll do my best to comply." Eagle repeated his proposal, "If you will furnish at least thirty qualified cavalrymen, we accept your offer." Art studied for a minute, "I can understand your request. I guess it would hard to recruit men locally for the Union, the sentiment being as it is at the present."

After dinner, they sat in the living room, discussing the agreement for a while, until Art finally said, "Alright if you present yourselves at Fort Upshire next week, we'll get things organized. Is that agreeable?"

"Yes Sir, we'll be there." They shook hands, Art bid the ladies goodby, and good luck, and departed.

Joe, Russ and Eagle spent the time getting ready. They each picked their favorite horse. For Joe, it was Kicker 111 now, curry combed, and brushed them good. Got down their saddles, saddled soaped, and shined them good. They didn't bother about clothes, since they would have to buy uniforms, including boots.

CHAPTER 41

The Wiseman Lancers

On Wednesday, they gathered their sons together informing them, "You are now the men of the house. It is your duty to look after your mother, help her in every way you can." Their wives, bravely embracing them goodby, they rode away to what ever fate had to offer them.

Arriving at Fort Upshire, the sentry at the gate pointed them to the Commanders office. Entering, a Sergeant asked, "How may I help you Gentlemen.?"

"We wish to see the commanding Officer please."

"Your name please."

"Wisemen."

"All of you have the same name?"

"Yes."

"Just a moment." He knocked on a door, entered. Art looked up, he said, "Sir there are three men out there to see you. They say their name is Wisemen." Smiling, Art said, "Kick them in the rear, and send them in." Grinning the Sergeant returned announced, "The Colonel will see you now. Go right in."

They entered, stood side by side grinning, "The Wiseman's reporting for duty." Art stood, shook hands, laughing said, "The next time you stand there, I expect a snappy salute, understand?" Still grinning, "Yes Sir." They replied in unison.

Art motioned for them to have a seat. "Well it's good to see you. We'll get right into it. First you must go over to supply, get your uniforms. That will come out of your first pay. I have already arranged for your quarters. An orderly will show you where they are. Change into those new uniforms, and report back here. I will have your troops assembled for inspection. I drained the pot for the best three Sergeants I have ever served with for you. You'll are already top heavy in rank, so you won't have a Lieutenant. "

When they returned from changing clothes, Art had the thirty men who had Volunteered to serve as their troops, standing at attention, in three ranks.

They approached, gave Art a brisk salute. He saluted back, turned to the troops, looked them up and down for a minute, before saying, "You have the privilege of serving with, not one, but three of the finest men it has been my privilege to meet. We served together, as U. S. Marshals. So I know personally, of their courage, and attention to duty. I now introduce them to you. From left to right. Captain Joe Wiseman, Captain Russ Wiseman and Captain Eagle Wiseman."

Sergeant Gene Randolf, Sergeant Paul Griffith and Sergeant Jim Beverley, will you step forward?" They moved out side by side. Art said, "Gentlemed, the finest three Sergeants in the 5th Cavalry at your service." The three Captains advanced side by side, each shaking hands with the Sergeant in front of him. They stood for a moment, looking at each other, directly eye to eye. In that moment a bond was formed, that would last through the war.

The Sergeants asked, "Sir would you like to inspect your Command?" Not waiting for an answer, they turned, one gave the Command to open ranks. Sergeant Randolf and Captain Joe Wiseman leading, they walked each rank, asking each man his name, looking him straight in the eye, shaking his hand.

After the inspection, the Colonel, with the order carry on, departed for his office. Sergeant Randolf asked, "Would you Gentlemen care for coffee?" Led the way to the mess hall. Over coffee, Joe asked Sergeant Randolf, "Have you rode with those men we just met.?" He replied, "From time to time yes. But I assure you they're expert Cavalrymen." Rus said, "Sitting face to face with men like you, I'm almost ashamed to admit our knowledge of soldiering likes a lot to be desired. As far as I'm concerned, when we're out on patrol, or what ever, you are in Command." Sergeant Griffith replied, "No sir, you command, we'll offer advice, if asked for. If you have been apprehending outlaws, and murderess, you won't have any trouble." The others agreed.

Eagle asked, "How soon do you suppose we can ride out together, to sort of getting acquainted?"

"Tomorrow morning would be fine. Why don't you check with the Colonel. He might already have something in mind.: "Fine we'll do that."

Over in the barracks, trooper Henry was saying, "Who ever gets in that Captain Eagles troop is going to get their belly full of fighting. He looks meaner than any of them Apaches we've been chasing. He seems nice and friendly, but did you see them eyes? He just looks at you, and you start shaking in your boots."

"Well if you ask me," Trooper Cunningham retorted, "Them others ain't no kind of pantywaist either. I heard the Colonel tell about them Rebel deserters they took care of. Right in front of their wives too."

"Yes trooper Jones cut in, how about all them outlaws and killers they chased through them canyons, dragged in with ropes around their necks? Why one time I heard, they shot up a whole town, that was trying to hang one of them, for a murder he didn't do." Sergeant Everely walked in about that time. "I see some of you laughing, but it's the truth. Not only that, they were ranchers, run thousands of cattle and horses. Just think about the rustlers they have put away." The tales went on, got bigger each time they were told. Which was good. Gave them more confidence in their Officers.

That evening at supper, Joe asked Art...the Colonel. They must remember not to call him Art...when they might take the troop out for a little training?...as much for themselves as the troops...He said, "I was going to tell you right after supper. But now is just as good. I've had a tip from our Civilian agent over there. A supply train carrying gold, ammunition and other supplies, is leaving Southern California, heading to Texas, in the next day or so. Your job is to see that train don't get very far into Arizona, let alone to Texas."

"Do you know what route they use?"

"Not exactly, it's somewhere just south of the Gila river. If you leave the first thing in the morning, that will give you time to scout it out."

"Fine, I'll alert the troops."

"You alert the Sergeants, they will have the troops mounted, and ready, before you get your boots on."

CHAPTER 42

The First Engagement for the Wiseman Lancers

Just after daylight, the troops were lined up beside their mounts. Each Sergeants by theirs, holding the reins of his Captains mount.

Captains, Joe, Russ and Eagle strode to them, with a bearing as much as like seasoned Officers as they could. Sergeant Randolf, called the troops to attention, then about faced, saluted, announced, "Sir the troops stand ready for your orders."

"Fine Sergeant, have them mount up." They each strode to their mounts, mounted, rode to the front. Gave the Command, "Lt turn, column of twos, forward." Art, watching out the window, smiled thought, "Well they carried that off right well." They rode with Captain Joe and Sergeant Randolf in front, side by side, ten troopers behind them. The others were lined likewise. Captain Russ and Sergeant Griffith, side by side, ten troopers behind them. Captain Eagle and Sergeant Beverley, with ten troopers behind them.

Out a ways, Captain Joe asked his Sergeant, "How did we do for three greenhorns?"

"Maybe green to the military ways, but nay greenhorns in any sense."

"Sergeant, you can tell the others, this was the first and last time for all that formality. We are a team I want to work that way. All that formal stuff is for the parade ground, as far as I'm concerned. Do you understand what I mean?"

"Indeed I do Sir, we'll get it straight."

"Another thing, from now on, I'm Joe or Captain. No more Sirs. That goes for the troopers as well."

"Got you Sir." They both laughed.

They stopped at noon, by a stream, to water the horses, and eat a quick lunch of beef jerky and hard tack. An hour before dark found them near the junction of the Colorado and Gila rivers, where they halted.

Captain Joe offered a suggestion, "Eagle why don't you and Sergeant Beverley scout across the border for a way, see if you can locate the trail the Californians use entering the Arizona Territory. It looks to me like we're sitting right on it, from the looks of all these tracks. Give a quick look, to see if that wagon train is any where near hear yet. We'll wait to you come back, before we decide on a camp site, and a good ambush place."

They returned, just as dark was setting in. Eagle reported, "The best we could tell, we're at the right place. No sign of the wagon train yet." Joe responded, "Well then, I think it's safe to have a small fire. Sergeant Randoph says one of our troopers always has coffee in his saddle bag. We'll have coffee, post sentries, kick the fire out, get some sleep."

The next morning, Eagle, Sergeant Beverley, taking two troopers to post as lookouts, rode back up the trail again. Finding no sight of the supply train yet, placed the look outs, rode back to camp to wait with the others.

Trooper Jones and Ridgely, thinking they heard riders, quickly hid behind a large clump of bushes. Soon two Grey Uniformed riders came down the trail, talking and laughing. The troopers let them pass, then rode out behind them, guns drawn. Startled the two turned, saw the blue uniforms, went to their guns, but stopped quickly, when a Command from trooper Jones ordered, "Hold it right there. Slowly unbuckle them gun belts, toss them over in them bushes. Now turn back around, ride slowly ahead." They walked their horses ahead as ordered until they broke out into the camp. Captain Eagle stepped forward, took the reins of both horses ordered, "Alright dismount." two troopers came over to cover them, as Captain Eagle asked, "Jones where in hell did you find these?"

"Well Captn' they just rode out on top of us. Only thing we knew to do, was bring them here."

"Ok, you did right."

Captain Joe began to question the Rebels. "How far back is the wagon train you're with?"

"Licking his lips, one said, "About a mile I'd guess."

"How many guards?"

"None now, they turned back just before we left them."

"Why?"

"We rode ahead to meet a detail of troops from Texas, to guard the wagons to where they're going."

"Where were you to meet these Texas troops?"

"They should have been here waiting for us." Joe looked at Eagle, who nodded his head barked, "C Troop, Mount up." Once mounted, they rode away to the East. To intercept the expected Confederate Texas troops.

About a half mile away, they spotted them, just leaving their night camp. Eagle ordered, "Draw sabers, charge!" The Texan's were surprised, and confused, it took a minute or two, for them to realize they were being attacked by this unexpected Union Cavalry troop. That short delay cost them dearly. Eagles troop was on them, sabers flying, dropped four out of the saddle, before the order to retreat, shouted by the Reb. Commander, sent them hightailing it back the way they came. Scattering in ever direction. Eagle led his troop in pursuit for away, before halting them. "Back to the wagons men. They're more important than a few Rebs." As they passed the four downed ones, Sergeant Everely asked, "What about these? "Leave 'em, their friends will come back for them after we're gone. Catch their horses though, we'll take them along."

Back at the wagons, they had finally arrived, Eagle reported their encounter with the Texan's. "After leaving four dead, they scattered like a flock of birds."

Captain Joe had ordered the drivers to climb down, had them searched for weapons, then returned to the drivers seat. They would still drive the wagons. The two captured guards had been searched, relieve of all weapons, allowed to mount their horse, but a trooper would lead each one.

When they were ready to start back to the Fort, Eagle, and his troop rode up ahead as scouts.

The wagons being so slow, required them to camp two nights before they reached Fort Upshire.

When they drove through the gate, they quickly acquired a audience, looking over their prize. Colonel McMagee congratulated them but said, "The next time, check it out. If there's gold and silver, take it out, destroy the rest. Don't take a chance on it being recaptured."

That night, in the barracks, trooper Jones, laughing, slapped his leg, "What did I tell you about that Captain' Eagle? Why he flew into them Texan's like ugly on a monkey. They never knew what hit 'em. Tucked their tails, run like a bugger was after 'em. Man, I'm telling you, I'm sticking right to his coat tail."

CHAPTER 43

Colonel McMagee received a dispatch, informing him that a Confederate battalion size force, was preparing to leave Southern Texas, heading for the Arizona Territory. Consulting his map, decided lightly defended Fort Claymore would be their objective.. He immediately dispatched the Wisemam Lancers plus another troop of Cavalry, with supplies, to reinforce the threatened Fort.

Arriving near the Fort before dark, Captain Eagle led his troop out to scout the area. He found the Rebel force encamped a short distance away. Ready to attack, come morning. He reported their position back to the others. The Officers discussed the situation. A decision was made for Captain Eagle to take his troop, infiltrate their pickets, destroy their wagons of supplies. Upon hearing the explosions, the rest of the column would attack.

Captain Eagle had four of the troopers, lash a keg of black powder behind his saddle. They cut strips from blankets, to muffle their horse's hooves. They rode slowly in as far as they dared. Captain Eagle, Sergeant Beverley and two troopers, each shouldered a keg of powder, sneaked up closer, then crawling on their bellies, easing the keg of powder along in front, slipped up under the first wagon. Noiselessly removed the bung,fron a keg of powder, poured out a portion. Leaving a keg there, skipping one wagon, crawled to the next, leaving a trail of black powder as they went, left a keg there. Skipping another wagon, leaving a trail of powder, left a keg there. Then working back to where the rest of the patrol waited, leaving a trail of powder as a fuse. Captain Eagle warned, "You boys watch your heads, hard to tell what kind of junk is going to be flying." He removed his hat, struck a match behind it, touched it to the trail of powder. Watched the little line of sparks, as they made their way to the wagons. Suddenly, there came a terrific explosion, fire and smoke leaping sky high. Debris raining everywhere.

Captain Joe ordered the remaining troops to move in. The Union occupants of the Fort, seeing the fire, and hearing the noise, rushed out. Seeing the Confederates, hurried to join the fight. To be caught so unawares, the Confederates fought viciously for a time, before those who could catch horses, began a hasty retreat, those on foot following. Union foot troops from the Fort, giving chase, but soon gave it up. It had been a sound defeat for the Confederates.

At the same time that Colonel McMagee ordered the Wiseman Lancers out to meet the first threat. He was making preparations to meet an even larger one.

A wire from the Western Commander, advised him that Confederate General, Harry Stappleton, had recruited a army of 2,500, and was about to leave San Antonio Texas, in November, for the Rio Grande, with orders to head North. On the way, capturing Fort Russel, before moving on to Santa Fe, the New Mexico Territories capitol, Albuquerque, and Fort Calhoun, guarding the Santa Fe Trail.

As it was, Colonel McMagee had plenty time. The Confederates had to cross 650 miles of desert. The heat, and scarcity of water, slowed the march considerably.

Stappleton, with the leading elment, while he waited for his strung out army to catch up. moved up the West side of the river, to a abandoned Union Fort. There he would establish a base of operation, for his move North. When the stragglers caught up, he immediately moved to capture, and occupy Fort Russel, 40 miles up river, that would be blocking his advance to the North.

Meanwhile Colonel McMagee's 5th Cavalry, reinforced with Colorado Mounted Volunteers, giving him a force, very near equal to that of the Confederates. With wagons loaded with supplies. The Wiseman Lancers on his left flank, a troop of Colorado Cavalry on the right flank, began his march South.

Reaching Fort Russel, Stappelton, learning from scouting reports, believed the Fort was too strong to attack, tried to draw them out for a fight. When they refused to leave the protection of the Fort, he led his troops across the river, to the East side, to continue his advance North.

He sent an advance party ahead, to take and occupy Albuquerque, to block any interference on his left flank. Reaching there, with the rest of the troops, decided to cross back to the West side of the river, so he could attack Santa Fe from the West, before moving on to Fort Calhoun, further to the East.

Crossing the river, was a bad decision. While most of his supply wagons were stranded in the river, he was attacked by McMagee's strong force, coming from the North. A vicious battle ensued, before Stappleton was able to break contact, with the aid of a Troop of Californians, on their way East, to link up with the Confederates. Leaving McMagee's Union force entangled with the Californians, Stappleton, having suffered a terrible loss in both men and supplies, moved on North, believing he could resupply in Santa Fe, and Fort Calhoun.

He did occupy Santa Fe. But his stay was short lived. A attack from Fort Calhoun sent him staggering back down the Rio Grande, leaving 1,700 of the 2,600 troops he started with behind, captured, wounded or dead. Santa Fe and Fort Calhoun would have to wait!

But Stappelton would try again. After resting a while, recruited another force, marched back to the New Mexico territory. Again suffering agonizing defeats.

Before leaving the West for the last time, he wrote, "The New Mexico Territory is not worth one quarter of the blood and treasure expended in it's conquest."

In less than a year from it's beginning the war in the New Mexico, and Arizona Territories, was over. Except for a few skirmishes Fifty years later they would become the 47 and 48 state in the Union.

CHAPTER 44

Joe, Russ and Eagle, returned home to a joyful reunion with their families. After a period of rest and recuperation, they retrieved their cattle and horses, that had been kept in safe keeping in Utah. Then began working to build their respective ranches back to pre-war standard, although Stella, Anita and Rose, had done a masterful job, holding things together.

The Wisemans

The Third Generation

Edwin, Dan and Steven, now back from college, advanced an idea to the families, on a way to expand the Wiseman holdings, in the New United States Territory of Arizona.

The coming of the railroad,** had made it possible to ship their beef to the far Eastern markets. Why not ship it in refined, more expensive products?

Edwin asked of his father, "Dad, how do you feel about spending some of that money, from your gold mining days, that's been molding away, there in the bank?"

"Well, for a good cause, I wouldn't mind at all. What do you have in mind?"

"I've been thinking, instead of shipping our beef on the hoof, how about nice juicy steaks, roasts, and other good beef products. Don't you think those Eastern folks would like that?"

"Laughing, his father said, "Maybe that college taught you something after all."

After extensive researching into the possibility, a site in the new capitol of Phoenix, was obtained, and construction began. In two years time, fine packaged meat products, from the Wiseman Meat Packing Company, were finding their way to tables, all across the country.

Dave and Steven managed the cutting, and packaging department. Edwin handled the sales and advertising. He traveled extensively, contacting wholesale companies, placing ads in newspapers, publicizing Wisemans Meat Products. Joe, Russ, and Eagle, moved their families into town,.... leaving their ranches in the hands of their capable foremen,... assumed equal status as President, Vice President, and Treasurer of the new Company. Stella, Anita, and Rose....after hiring capable employees handled the business end.

The Company grew so fast, that after two years, an addition had to be added to the meat handling department. Everyone was pleased with their job, and their contribution to the Company, except Dave. With claustrophobia, and his Indian Heritage,... the love of the outdoors,.... working against him, he had to find a way out. Reading an article in the Phoenix Post, describing a Cavalry attack on a Apache strong hold, lead by Colonel Art McMagee, gave him food for thought.

Remembering the stories related by his father, and uncles, about their service with the Colonel, left him a little surprised, he was still in the Army. Working on the old adage...nothing beats a failure, but a good try....Wrote the Colonel a letter, giving a short 'resumae' of his name, education, and the reason for his desire to enter the Army.

Ten days later, he received a reply from Colonel McMagee stating,

Mr. Dave Wiseman:

It was a nice surprise hearing from you. I remember meeting you, and your cousins as young men, while visiting your parents, at the beginning of the war. It's hard to believe, that time passes so quickly. You were twelve or thirteen years old at that time. Sorry you have become dissatisfied working in the family business. I had somewhat the same feeling, that's the reason I remained in the Army.

If you are seriously interested in a career in the Army, I'd be happy to discuss the matter with you, if you wish to make the trip up here to the Fort.

Thank you for your interest in the Army.

Art McMagee, Colonel U. S. Army

Dave informed his parents of his decision, to go talk with Colonel McMagee. His mother was against it, but withheld any comments. Eagle, feeling great pride said, "If that's really what you want to do, listen to the Colonel, he speaks with a straight tongue. His advice will help you make the right decision."

CHAPTER 45

Dave took the train to Santa Fe, caught a supply wagon to Fort Calhoun. He asked for, and was directed to the Colonels office. Inside, he informed the Sergeant he would like to speak to the Colonel. The Sergeant informed him, "Just give a rap on the door there, and go right in. He found the Colonel studying a pile of reports. He stood, came around his desk smiling, offering his hand said, "You must be Dave Wiseman?"

"Yes Sir."

"You are a complete image of your father. One of my most trusted friends."

" Thank you Sir, I'm often told that I resemble him."

"How is he?"

"Well Sir, I think he'd much rather be standing here, than cooped up in that office." Laughing the Colonel said, "I know how right you are."

"Well, you want to talk about joining the Army, is that right?"

"Yes Sir, I didn't like being cooped up either."

"Has old Eagle told you what a mean task master I am."

"Just the opposite Sir. He thinks very highly of you. Instructed me to listen to you very carefully."

"W

n I receive your letter, it started me thinking. You grew up around the Apaches, ,m,munderstand their ways and habits. Army commanders out here are under a good deal of pressure to bring them to heal...so to speak...but they are so elusive, not a great deal of progress has been made."

"With your education, I can offer you a Commission. The Army is always interested in educated young men, to fill the Officer Corps. Would you be interested in accepting a Commission as Chief Scout, with the rank, and pay of Captain?"

"You, at your discretion, could chose to wear the uniform, or not. I would prefer for you to wear the buckskins, to set you apart from the other Officers. Of course you would need a uniform for special occasions."

"Is it because I'm Indian, you feel I wouldn't be accepted as a regular Cavalry Officer?"

"No not at all, there are German, French, Spanish, and other nationalities, serving as Officers. It is to protect you from other Officers giving you orders, trying to pass their duty off on you. It's Something all young Officers has to put up with. It happened to me. There were two Officers, one step senior to me, kept harassing me, until I rebelled...a little too physically I'm afraid.. causing a egotistic, self-serving General, to ask for my resignation."

"Have you made up your mind, or do you need more time to think it over?"

"I'm ready now. What do I have to do now?"

"I'll swear you in now, then you go over to the supply room, purchase your uniforms. An orderly will meet you there, take you to your quarters. I'll introduce you to the troops, and Officers at reveille in the morning."

At War with the Indian in the West

The next morning, after Reveille, the troops were ordered to stand fast, for a word from the Colonel. The Colonel, with Dave beside him, walked to the front of the formation. Looking over the assembled troops, the colonel said, "I won't hold you but a few minutes. I would like to introduce Captain David Wiseman, the Chief Scout for this region." The troops, and Officers were a little taken back at the way Dave was dressed. Buckskins from shoulder to toe. A beaded band around his head. The Colonel continued, "Some of you older men might remember Daves father, Captain Eagle Wiseman, from the late war. Well Dave is a chip off the old block. He's promised he will go after the Apaches, just like Captain Eagle went after the Rebs. He informed me he had a little speech he wanted to make. I'll only last about an hour".... sighing erupted throughout the ranks... Dave stepped forward, looked the assembled troops over smiling said, "Howdy." stepped back, to roars of laughter. The formation was dismissed for chow.

CHAPTER 46

Dave walked toward the mess hall, a Lieutenant fell in step by him. After a moment he said, "If you'll pardon me Sir, I'm Lieutenant Jim Everely. I served with your father, throughout the late war. When I learned you were his son, I wanted to serve with you." Dave stopped, offering his hand, "My father talked quite often about a Sergeant Everely he was fond of. Would you by chance, be any kin to him?"

"The one and the same Sir. It was your father who pinned this Lieutenant board on my shoulder."

"What I've learned about your service together, it was well deserved."

"Thank you Sir. But right now, I'm not sure I want it."

"For what reason?"

"I was about to ask you, if it is possible, for me to work with you, being a Lieutenant." Laughing Dave asked, "You mean you want to wear buckskins too?" Lieutenant Everely laughing also said, "Yes Sir, If that's what it takes, and even if I have to, take a Sergeant rating again."

"Let me check with the Colonel, on one condition."

"What's that Sir?" "You drop the word Sir, use Captain, or David, when addressing me." The Lieutenant began laughing heartily. "Would you believe that's exactly the same order your father gave me?"

"What did you say to him?"

"Yes Sir." Both laughing, they went off to see the Colonel.

The Colonel approved the arrangement. Everely could keep his rank. At the next formation, when they were seen dressed alike, one trooper was heard to say, "Well I guess the whole 5th Cavalry is going to start wearing buckskins. And you know I'd like that, all except the hat. I feel kind of naked without my hat." Another trooper shot back, "If my head was as bald as yours, I'd keep my hat on too. It blinds the whole troop, when you take your hat off, to wipe your brow. All that energy used to make them pretty curls in your hair, is just wasted. Mine goes to my brain. That's what makes me a better Cavalryman than you. See who rides up front, and carries the Guidon don't you?"

"You got that all wrong. They give that little stick, with a flag on it, to the biggest dummy in the troop. Ask any of these guys."

"You go riding into a bunch of Apaches with a stick, not a rifle."

"That's what makes it an honor. Takes a brave man to carry the Guidon." The order, "Quiet in the ranks." Ended the repartee.

CHAPTER 47

Dave and Jim checked several reports on bands of Apaches, raiding farms along the Santa Fe trail. The elusive Apaches were gone before they arrived.

They were leading Captain Reynolds B troop on patrol, south of the trail, when they were halted by a rider, coming fast, waving his hat to attract their attention. He pulled his mount up short in front of the patrol. Blood running down the side of his face, incoherently trying to tell them what had happened. Dave moved his horse over beside him, holding up his hand to halt his talking, talking slow, and softly, finally got him settled down. In halting words, he told him the Apaches had attacked their wagon train, killing several people, retreated, carrying away his wife, and their small daughter. Dave said, "Let the Doc look at that wound on your head, then lead us to the site."

"Wound be-dammed," he shouted. Turning his horse, spurring it savagely, headed back the way he came. Dave, Jim, and the troop right behind him.

Reaching the site of the disaster, they found the surviving men, already digging graves to burry the dead. Captain Reynolds ordered some of his men to dismount, and help. Dave looking out asked, "Is those men coming in, with you?" Someone answered, "Yes, one of them is the boss, and scout for our wagons. They left immediately, trying to follow the Indians. Looks like they didn't have much luck."

When they reached the wagons, Dave asked, "Which one of you is in charge?"

"I am. My name is Randy Cavendish. Them devils came out from behind them rocks, and brush, hit us before we knew what was happening. It was over in ten minutes."

"They killed five people, grabbed Franks wife, and daughter, left in a cloud of dust."

"We tried to follow, but lost sight of them in the rocks and gullies."

"Where are you headed for?"

"California."

"There's a town, Sandstone, up ahead about two miles. When you've taken care of everything here, why don't you go on there, make your camp, and wait for word from us." Frank stepped forward stating, "I'm going with you."

"I'm sorry Sir, I know how you feel. But it's best if you remain with your friends. We'll get back to you soon as possible."

Dave and Jim led the troop out in the desert two miles or so, before halting them. Dave called the Captain aside, explaining what he had in mind, "This is a good place for you to rest the troop. You have the advantage of the high ground, if trouble arises. Jim and I are going to do some scouting. It might take a while, so don't get too restless. If we find something, or don't, in a reasonable length of time, we'll check back with you. Is this agreeable with you?"

"We'll be here when you get back, whenever that is."

CHAPTER 48

Dave and Jim searched up and down several small canyons. Finding plenty tracks, but they were so mixed, going off in all directions, they were unable to get a definite reading from them. They were about two hours away from the troop, when the horses began pulling at the reins, trying to turn to their left. Jim, pulling his horse back straight observed, "These animals smell water. Seems to be over that way." Pointing to the left. "Let's give them their head, but move slowly."

He had just topped a rise far enough to see over it, when suddenly he stopped, pulled back on the reins, backing his horse back down the slope. Answering the question in Daves eyes, and grinning said, "We've found them. Their village is about two or three hundred yards beyond this hill, set back in a grove of trees." They dismounted, ground tied the horses, crawled back up far enough, they could lay on their bellies, and see over the top.

They watched for a while, before Jim said, "I don't see a brave anywhere do you?"

"No, I haven't. We might be in trouble. Let's get out of here, find another place to watch from, we don't want a bunch of braves crawling up our back. They could be anywhere behind us, or taking a nap." Grinning, Jim said, "You're the expert. Didn't the Spanish teach them to take a siesta during the hot afternoon?"

"Yeah, but maybe this bunch ain't sleepy, or got a massacre going someplace Let's not take a chance." They moved back, made a wide detour, came in on top of the hill opposite the one they were on. Dave observed, "This is a better watching post. You can see more of the village through the trees."

They watched the activity down in the village, until late in the afternoon. Jim started chuckling, "Them ornery braves were taking a nap." They were leading their horses to water, took them back to the picket line. Began gathering around the large iron pot, that was hanging over the fire, for their evening meal. An older woman, detached herself from the group, carrying food, went to one of the tepees, untied the door flap, entered with the food. She stayed only a few minutes, came out, retied the door, made her way back to the group. Dave watching her movements, tapped Jim on the arm, nodded in her direction said, "We know where the captives, and the horses are, we can make our rescue plan. Here's what I've come up with. Then you can tell me what you think."

"It's about an hour, back to the troops. You ride back there, bring them here to this point. We wait until midnight, or a little later. You can pick the best rider in the troop, taking two halters with you, find your way around to the picket line, slip the halter on two of the ponies. Give me time to crawl up behind the tepee, where the captives are. When you are ready, cut the picket rope, you and the rider mount up, chase the other ponies, down the middle of the village. The confusion should give me time to slit the back of the tepee, grab the woman, and little girl, race back here. The Cavalry can ride in shoot up the place, making more confusion, before withdrawing. We all can rejoin the troop, leaving the Apaches to lick their wounds." Jim was shaking his head. "While you were talking, a vision of your father came to me, standing in front of his troop, outlining his plan of attack. He couldn't have done it better. And I wouldn't presume to add anything to your plan."

CHAPTER 49

The troop rode into Sandstone, with a smiling young Angie Swanson, sitting in the saddle in front of Dave. A even more happy Frank Swanson, that rushed out to help his wife Dorthy down from behind Jim.

Handing Angie down to her mother, Dave informed the leader of the wagon train, Randy Cavendish, the troop would accompany them to the California line, before returning to the Fort

Dave and Jim, continued escorting wagon trains, and skirmishing with the Apaches for the next year, until Colonel McMagee called his officers in for a conference. "Gentlemen we have been ordered up North. The Sioux, Cheyenne, Comanche, Arapho, and Shoshone, have set aside their fighting with each other, banding together, in the largest uprising to date.

"But before we go, I want to spank the Apaches butt real good. I see some of you are laughing at my choice of words. Kind of sounds like were talking about school boys, don't it. Well I meant for it to be a bit humorous, to offset this moving news."

"Our Chief Scouts have devised a plan to ambush them good."...one of the Apache;s own favorite games..."We're going to send A and B troop up North, into Colorado, making a big show of leaving. They will be joined by the like number of Colorado Mounted Cavalry. They will stand ready to charge back here, when the fireworks start."

"While the Apaches are watching them, two troops of Cavalry will infiltrate here by night, from Russel.... They're patrolling up this way now.... Forming a pincher to catch the Apaches in the middle. Now I realize there are some if's mixed in here." "The Apaches, have attacked this Fort numerous times, without any success at all."

"What we're banking on is, when they see the movement North, it will leave the Fort weak enough, they can use a large enough force, and take it. Ok, questions, or suggestions?" From Doctor Graves, "What about the women, and children?"

"They will be barricaded in that large root cellar. The kids will have plenty apples to eat."

"Once they start their attack, we'll hit them hard and fast. No Indian will get inside the Fort. Any thing else? Ok there will be a meeting of Commanders tomorrow at noon, to coordinate positions, and times. Dave and Jim will liaison between the two forces."

On the second night after the trap was set, there was evidence the Apaches had taken the bait. Lookouts reported numerous camp fires over to the west. The laisison Officers alerted the unit Commanders, to expect an attack at first light.

They came, in two columns, yelling, and firing, to create all the confusion possible. Splitting columns as they approached the Fort, one to each side. Before one complete circle could be made, with bugles sounding the charge, They were hit hard by the charging Cavalry. Their loss being so great on that first charge, the wise old Chief Ornes realizing he had been ambushed, signaled for a retreat. The Cavalry withdrew to the Fort, to await the next attack.

Before long they came slowly riding back. Chief Ornes in front, holding his lance straight up. The Command was quickly given, "Hold your fire, they're after their dead." The Chief sat stoically in the saddle, until they had all been lifted across their ponies back. Turned his pony, slowly leading them away. It had been the biggest Apache defeat, since Colonel McMagee had been at Fort Calhoun.

CHAPTER 50

The Move North

One week after... spanking the Apaches,.... Colonel McMagee had the unit on the 250 mile trek across the South Eastern tip of Colorado, to Fort Claymore in Western Kansas. A cavalry unit from Fort Russel would move in to Fort Calhoun to replace the departing 5th Cavalry, and the remaining Infantry, to guard the Santa Fe trail against the Apaches.

With the slow moving wagons, and progress of barely 10 to 12 miles a day, it took a long month of dusty travel, before they reached Fort Claymore. The were replacing a Unit that had been shifted hurriedly to Montana, because of the Sioux threat from South Dakota.

They were to learn what the word 'ambush' really meant from the Comanche. They were masters at tantalizing you with a small party, leading you into a much larger one, where, if you were lucky, enough survived to carry the dead back to the Fort. They did it in so many variations, and places you wouldn't expect. The Army couldn't seem to catch on.

Dave and Jim led patrols, chasing raiding parties, fighting off attacks on wagon trains crossing the prairie for a year.

Dave, leading a troop of Cavalry in pursuit of a band of Comanches that was raiding, killing, and burning farms to the West of the Fort, came upon a farm where most of the buildings was still smouldering. While the Captain led his troop on, trying to overtake the Indians, Dave stayed behind, to make sure there was no one left alive or injured. There were none. The occupants had been in the burning home.

He continued on following the troop. About a mile, while passing a small copse of trees, something caught his eye. Riding in the trees a way, spotted an Indian pony. He rode toward it, and the pony never ran or even moved from the spot.

He dismounted walked on close. Lying on the ground was a young Indian girl. Holding a knife in her hand, fear in her eyes, tried moving away. Holding up his hand, reached to the scabbard at his side, pulled his knife, laid it on the ground, trying to allay her fear. After a while she relaxed, lay the knife she was holding, down beside her. Dave walked on to her, bending over, could she was badly hurt. Taking the hand, now free of the knife, placed it over the other arm. Talking softly he looked close, to see blood staining her shirt. He gently removed her hand, felt the arm she had been holding. It was broken between the shoulder and elbow. The blood was coming from a cut on her shoulder. That arm would have to be set before swelling set in. He pondered for a minute on just what to do. She would have to be moved from here. Remembering the burnt out farm back behind, made up his mind.

He removed his shirt, bent over, slipping the arms under the broken arm, and around her neck, tying them to make a sling. He gently coaxed her to her feet, wincing himself, at the pain showing on her face, but never uttering a sound. He led her to her pony, lifted her up, mounted his horse, taking the reins from her pony, walked out of the trees, and back to the farm.

Dave rode right into the barn, like other small out buildings has escaped the torch. He lifted the girl down, put the horses in a stall. Saying to himself, "That arm has to come first." Picked a place near the door, piled up hay, covered it with saddle blankets, hanging on a rail, led her over, helped her sit so she could lean back. He found a thin piece of board, shaped two splints to fit her arm. Removed his shirt, tore it into strips to bind the splint with. Taking a deep breath, he knelt in front of her, and by hand signals tried to show her what he was going to do. Her eyes following every movement. He couldn't tell if she understood or not. He reached over took a firm grip on each section of the arm, holding his breath, gave sudden pull, bringing the two pieces together again. She fainted, laying her head back against the pillow of hay he had fashioned. Quickly he applied the splint, bound it together, made another sling from the remaining part of his shirt, gently laid her arm in it. Remembering seeing a spring house, he went there, found a tin cup hanging on a post, filled the cup, returned to find her still lying as he left her. Removing his neckerchief, wet it in the cool water, bathed her face, until she came to. Frightened again, she started to struggle. He gently laid his hand on her arm smiling, shaking his head no. he offered her the cup for a drink. She nodded, took it, drank heartily.

Dave next examined the cut place again. It wasn't as bad as he first thought, but it would have to be cleaned thoroughly. He had nothing to put on it, but if kept clean, it should heal good. He built a fire outside the door, went back to the spring house, found a small pot, filled it with water, returned, placed it over the fire. When it heated enough, using his neckerchief again bathed the wound good. When he finished, she was sleeping.

While she slept, he scouted around for something to eat. In one of the small out buildings, he found a potato bin. Gathering up a few, resumed his search. In another building, to his disbelief a smokehouse, with a few scraps of smoked meat hanging from hooks from the rafters. He chose a small piece of ham, returned to the barn. Laughing to himself, "I'm not the best cook around, but

I'm a stomp down good one." He fixed a stew with the ham and potatoes, placed it over the fire, sat down for a rest.

He sat resting, and watching over the sleeping girl. She was quite beautiful. A small, round sweet face, long black hair, not braided, but falling around her neck to her shoulder. What was she doing there? She is not Comanche. Must be Pawnee, captured in a raid by the Comanches. Possibly the ones that did this burning here.

She began to stir, moaning a little. Jerking awake, she sat up, remembered where she was, began feeling the hurt arm. Puzzled at the splint. Dave had been watching her movements, from out of her sight, began to feel satisfied she was going to be alright. He moved around in her sight smiling, pantomimed eating. She smiled for the first time, nodding her head that she understood. Dave had found tin plates in the spring house, probably lids for something. He dipped her out a plate of stew, laid a wooden spoon in it, that he had carved out while she slept. Got another cup of water, took it in to her. Again smiling, she held it up, smelling of it. She sit the plate on her lap, picked up the wooden spoon, looked at it. Looking at Dave, she spooned up a small bite, tasted of it, then quickly ate the plate full, handed it back to Dave. He refilled the plate, gave it back. She ate it more slowly, then set the plate aside.

They camped there a week. Dave wanted to be sure the arm was ok. He watched it closely for swelling, or redness. At the end of the week, she began pointing to her pony, and to the East. Dave figured her home must be that way. He led the mounts outside, lifted he up, handed her the reins, then mounted himself, motioned for her to lead off.

After a two hour ride, she stopped on top of a knoll, pointed to her village. Several tepees nestled along the river. They set there together looking, for quite some time, before Dave motioned for her to go ahead. She seemed sad for a moment, then nudged her pony on. Out a ways she stopped, turned to look back for a minute, turned again, rode on, never looking back again. Dave sat there, a little sad himself. He turned to head back to the Fort, thinking the Colonel will have me before a Court Marshal for desertion.

Arriving at her village, was a cause for celebration, she being the Chiefs daughter. The celebration lasted until one big strong brave, came up to her. He looked the arm over, taking a hold of the sling, with a yank said, "Mans shirt, where is he?" A resounding slap, sent him stomping away, ending the gaiety, and making an unknown enemy for Dave.

Daves reception was a little more congenial. After hearing about his experience, Colonel McMagee said, "Well you have already made a step in the new direction. We have orders to start a peace keeping program. Inviting leading

Chiefs in to talk peace, listen to their demands. Sending our findings to Washington for evaluation."

"In my opinion we might just as well send them to Tim Buck Do. All they do is make a bunch of promises, then break them, causing the fighting to become more vicious."

CHAPTER 51

The Ambush

Two months after Daves rescue of the Pawnee girl, he and Jim were on a mission to Comanche villages, with orders to try to persuade their Chiefs to an up coming peace conference, to be held at Fort Claymore, with a General from Washington in attendance.

They were fording a small stream, that was lined with thick brush, and trees on both sides. As they came out of the trees on the far side, they were immediately surrounded by five Pawnee braves. The leader of the group was Grizzly, his unknown enemy. Named after the bear, for his mean temperament. With Dave and Jim in the middle, they headed for their village. Once there, Dave and Jim were each tied with their hands behind a post. Dave looking over the people who had crowded around, curious to see the captives, locked eyes with his friend, the girl he had helped. With Grizzly agitating them, the onlookers were becoming loud, and unruly.

In just a few minutes the onlookers began to part, making way for Chief Running Fox and his daughter. Stopping in front of the two stakes, he stated, "Cut them loose. These men are guest of the Pawnee. No harm is to come to them. Pointing to Dave said, "This one saved Wild Flowers life. He is honored among all Pawnee." Turning to Dave and Jim announced, "We powwow tonight, my tepee." Holding Wild Flowers arm, they walked back the way they had come. Watching them go, Dave said, "Well I finally know her name. She looks more lovely now, than she did when I left her up on that knoll. Jim said, "Dave my boy, I have a feeling the Cavalry will be losing it's Chief Scout, and me my best friend, before long."

"No Jim, we'll always be friends, no matter what happens."

The Challenge

Later that evening, Dave and Jim were walking through the village, when they saw Wild Flower coming from the river with a pail of water. Dave rushed to her, took the pail. Both smiling, walked on together. Suddenly Grizzly appeared in front of them. Looking daggers at Dave, threw his lance in the ground in front of Dave. With another angry look, stamped off. Jim came up to them, a deep furrow on his face. Dave laughing asked, "What does this mean?"

"Don't laugh, you have been challenged to a fight."

"Suppose I don't want to fight?"

"You will be dishonored among all Pawnees, and so will he. You can live with your plight, but he can't. To overcome his dishonor, he must kill you."

"What about the Chiefs warning?"

"Sometimes it's not so good to be a Chief. It will pain him greatly, but their honor code requires him to stand by his man."

"What kind of fight must take place?"

"Knives, with a length of rawhide held by each ones teeth. If you drop the rawhide, without being wounded, or killed, you are the dishonored one, he is not."

Wild Flower, with a horrifying look on her face, had been listening. She knew the rule of course. She laid a hand on Daves arm whispering, "Hurry, go now. He kill many men." Dave helped her on to her tepee with the water, patted her arm, and he and Jim walked away to talk it over some more. Jim asked, "Surely you're not going through with this idiotic scheme are you?"

"What you don't know is, that I'm a pretty good knife fighter myself. In school I was the champion dueler. I know that is different, longer knives, protective apparel, and all that. But I learned a few tricks. What is the procedure, how does it start?"

"You stand face to face, the rawhide throng just long enough, that you can reach other, between your teeth. Each man has a second to begin with. Their job is to throw the knife, both at the same time, so it sticks in the dirt between each man's feet, and the fight is on. Each man finessing, to grab his knife first. You must watch carefully. A trick is to let the other man bend over first, so you can kick dirt in his eyes. Well you know what that means. A man coming at you with a large knife, and you can't see. Another thing, he will probably have his upper body greased with animal fat, making it hard to get a hold on him. I'll see if I can find Wild Flower, have her get us a little of some kind."

The Duel

Dave and Jim were notified the contest would begin at sunrise the next day. Jim watched as Dave did a series of limbering up exercises, that night. It had been a long time since he had done anything like dueling, which dictates you have a quick supple body, and legs. He exercised until he was good and tired...he would do a few more in the morning...lay down on a buffalo robe, for a good nights sleep.

The next morning a Brave stuck his head in said, "You come." Dave removed his shirt. Jim rubbed him down good with some of the tallow Wild Flower had given him. He did a few quick exercises. Smiling said, "Trainer, shall we go to meet the challenge of the new day?"

"Now don't you get too feisty. Remember caution is the key word for today."
They left the tepee, walked through spectators that were forming a ring for the
fighters. Grizzly was already there, looking every bit like his namesake. His
second handed him the rawhide throng to inspect, then to Dave. Stretching it,
felt it was strong enough, handed it back. A Brave stepped forward with two,
just alike hunting knives, gave Dave his choice first. A courtesy afforded the
challenger. Dave picked one, hefted it. It seemed to be well balanced. Grizzly
took his, did the same testing routine. Next he handed Dave one end of the
throng, instructing him to place it between his teeth, then to Grizzly. They were
instructed to hand their knives to their seconds, step back until the throng was
taunt, and get ready.

The signal was given, both knives stuck in the ground at the same time. They
began circling, each looking for that one instant the other was off guard.
Suddenly, Dave jumped forward, caught his knife between his feet, kicking the
other one away at the same time. Jumped again, catching the knife in his hand.
All Grizzly could do was grab for the knife hand, then it became a wrestling
match between two very strong men. They were on the ground, rolling over and
over. Then standing. Grizzly holding on to Daves knife hand. The next time
they came to a standing position, Dave, pulled hard, falling to his back. With his
feet turned Grizzly a flip over his body, quickly rolled on top with his knife
blade making a small scratch under his chin, bringing a little blood. All it would
take now, was push the blade on in, and Grizzly would join his ancestors. Dave
looked him steady in the eye for a moment, then climbed to his feet, threw the
knife to the ground, started walking away. Grizzly jumped up, grabbed the knife,
started for Daves back, when a shot rang out. Grizzly fell forward mortally
wounded, with a bullet through his chest. Chief Running Fox stood holding a
smoking gun in his hand said, "That was for his dishonor to the Pawnee people.
He could have lived with the first dishonor, but not the second. He is not to be
buried in the honored ancestral burying ground." Turning he walked away.

The PowWow was held that night. Chief Running Fox gave his promise to
attend. As they rode back to the Fort, Dave said, "Jim you were right in one
sense. I think I'm going to resign my Commission."

"What do you have in mind to do after that?"

"I'm not quite sure. I have some more thinking to do." The subject was
dropped, and they talked about the duel the rest of the way in.

CHAPTER 52

The Decision

Dave pondered his decision for two weeks, before finalizing it. He went in to see the Colonel asked, "Sir may I talk to you on a personal matter?"

"Yes of course Dave, what's on your mind.?"

"Sir I wish to resign my Commission."

"What are your plans?"

"Well Sir, I wish to get married."

" David you don't have to resign to do that. Who is the lucky girl?"

"She doesn't know it yet." Laughing the Colonel said, "Well that's some kind of confidence. You didn't say who she was."

"Her name is Wild Flower, a lovely Pawnee Princess."

"I understand the resignation part now."

"What kind of work do you plan to enter. Go back to the family business?"

"No Sir, not just now anyway."

"With your education there will be all sort of jobs opening up in the Indian Affairs Department. Had you considered that?"

"No Sir, I've been a part of killing them. I don't want to be a part of shoving them off to some rock pile to starve to death. Another thing, this new policy of "kill them all, even their dogs. Destroy their homes, they'll have to go to the reservation." Don't make any sense. Some bright Judge Advocate General got his words mixed up. If you destroy the people, while destroying their homes, who the devil is left to put on a reservation?"

"Well, you had better run for Congress, we need men like you up there, instead of you scratch my back, and I'll scratch yours kind." Laughing Dave said, "Maybe both of us should go up there, and kick a few butts."

"If you're serious, write it up, giving the date you wish to leave, place it on my desk, and I'll sign it, push it through." Dave thanked him, saluted, left a stunned Colonel shaking his head.

CHAPTER 53

The Unexpected Change

Until a month ago, Dave had never thought about leaving the Army. In fact there had been a hidden ambition popping up in his mind. Serve thirty years, retire with an elevated rank..a Colonel maybe, General no!...That option would no longer be available just as soon as he signed the paper he was writing.

He placed his signed resignation on Colonel McMagees desk, looked at it with a moment of hesitation, picked up his bag of personal articles, left not looking back.

He made the circuit, telling his friends goodby. It was especially hard when he came to Jim. But they would be visiting each other as often as possible. All finished, he went to the corral, saddled his horse, rode to the front gave a snappy Military salute to the Flag for the last time, turned rode away toward the Pawnee village, and his new immediate future.

Wild Flower was surprised, and happy to see him. When he had dismounted she ran to him, and they walked around the village laughing and talking.

Before the sunset on that day, Dave had asked Chief Running Fox for permission to marry his daughter. Permission was granted, a date was set for two days from this day, two hours before sunset.

The wedding was a simple affair, performed according to the law, and custom of the Pawnee tribe. A tepee was erected beside that of the Chief. At the specified time, Dave and Wild Flower walked between two rows of well wishers, and giggling young girls, entered their new home, dropped the door flap. After consummation, they were man and wife.

Dave spent three years, helping the tribe through crisis after crisis. Finally the push to move the tribe to a reservation, forced him to consider taking his wife to his home in the Arizona Territory.

He went to the Fort, spoke to the Doctors wife, Mrs Elsie Morgan. Major and Mrs Morgan had always been close friends, while he served at the Fort. He wanted to know if Mrs Morgan would take Wild Flower shopping for western type clothes suitable for traveling. He planned on making the trip by stage coach, rather than the train. There was still a lot of prejudice against Indians traveling on public conveyances, especially trains, since they still attacked them.

Mrs Morgan was happy to do as he asked. She had met Wild Flower, on their visits to the Fort, and thought highly of the lovely young lady.

CHAPTER 54

Back to Arizona and Home

Dave and Wild Flower arrived in Phoenix, caught a carriage out to the plant. They stood on the street awhile, to let an awed Wild Flower take in the sights. Looking op to the large sign atop the building she asked, "Is that your name up there? Is this all yours?"

"It's your name too sweetheart. But no, it's not all mine. It belongs to the whole family, which you're a part of. You are a wealthy young lady."

"Come, lets go inside." A fancy dressed doorman met them asking, "May I help you folks?"

"Yes I'm David Wiseman. I would like to see my mother, Mrs. Rose Wiseman, or my father Mr. Eagle Wiseman." The doorman looked at him strangely for a minute before saying, "I'll take you to Mrs. Wisemans office." He led them to a door, pushed a button, the door opened. He motioned them inside a small room. Suddenly the room started upward. Frightned, Wild Flower grabbed Davids arm. He laughed, "This pony does all kind of tricks. Watch this ...Whoa!" The room stopped.... "You see?"

When the door opened, their escort pointed, "The second door on the right. What shall I do with your luggage?"

"Just leave it in the lobby for the time being."

At the door, Dave gave a light rap, opened it, led Wild Flower in by the arm. Dave couldn't believe the lovely grey haired lady that stood was his mother. He counted the years quickly. It had been sixteen years since he had seen her. But it didn't take her long to know who he was. With tears building in her eyes, she ran to him, embracing, and kissing his cheek over, and over. Pushing him back, she said, "David, why in the world didn't you let me know you were coming?"

"Well mother, it was a sudden change of mind. We just packed up and left." Pulling Wild Flower to his side, "This is Wild Flower my wife." Embracing her, his mother said, "Where did you find such a lovely girl way out West."

"I combed the Prairie, until I found her. She is a Pawnee princess. Her father is Chief of the Pawnee Nation in Kansas."

"Will you excuse me a minute, I'll tell Anna, my secretary, I'm leaving for the day. After you see Anita and Stella, we'll go home where can talk."

Rose had a carriage brought around to the front, David luggage was loaded, and they left for home. Rose rode along quietly, her hands folded on her lap.

David wanted to ask why every one seemed so sad back at the plant, and where his father was, but didn't want to break in on his mothers reverie.

At home, His mother asked the house keeper to bring coffee, while they got settled. When the coffee arrived, his mother leaned back in her chair, wiped her eyes, speaking in a low tone said. "I know you noticed the veil of sadness at the office, and no men around. The sad news is, they are all dead. Three years ago, there was a terrible explosion and fire in the packing department. They were all were caught, couldn't get out, died of suffocation, before the firefighters could get to them. They didn't burn, but died just the same."

"All five of them?"

"Yes, all five. We tried to get word to you, but nobody seem to know your whereabouts. The Army said you had resigned, and didn't know your location."

"What do you ladies plan to do?"

"We hoped you would return, take over running it."

"Mother I don't to be discourteous, pigheaded, or what. But I want nothing to do with it. Why not sell out. I'm sure there are business people who would be interested in it."

"Oh yes, we've had several offers already."

"Why not sell it. Let's move back to the ranch?"

"I'm not sure I could stay there with your father gone."

"Well, I guess I can see your point. I suppose Aunt Anita, and Aunt Stella feel the same?"

"We have talked about it, and I believe they do."

"I want to take Wild Flower to the ranch, show her where I was raised. Then to Gila Springs, where the Wiseman tribe originated, while we decide where we want to settle down."

"I'm afraid you won't find things the same there either. Ed, Helen, Maggie, Ben and Jenny passed away four years ago. Your father, and your uncle Joe sold the ranch."

"Anyway I want to go."

"Why don't you, and Aunt Anita, and Aunt Stella talk some more. Maybe by the time we get back, we all can make a decision."

"We'll think about it." She looked at Wild Flower, smiling asked, "My dear, do you mind if we call you Flo? It is short for Flower. Wild Flower is a beautiful name, just a little long." Flo laughed, "I've tried to get him to do that. But he refused, maybe you can get him to change his mind."

"Well, come on Flo, let's go see about our luggage, and more travel arrangements."

"Do we have to go on that awful, bumpy old stage coach? Do they have horses here?" Dave, and his mother, both laughed. "Maybe we can go rustle a couple." Rose said, "Why don't you take the carriage out to the ranch with your luggage? You can rustle a couple good horses out there."

"No wonder this outfit had grown so much, with business heads like you, that work around here. Just joking mother. I never thought about that."

They made the ranch just as it was getting dark. Uncle Joe's foreman Clyde, still there, made them welcome.

CHAPTER 55

A Journey Into The Past

Before bedtime, Dave made them a bedroll with an extra set of clothes. Borrowed some eating, and cooking utensils, enough food for a week, which would go on the pack horse. Every thing was made ready for an early start the next morning. After breakfast they were off. As they rode along, Dave pointed to large herds of cattle grazing, that belonged to the ranch. Told Flo about when he was a boy, he was allowed to go along on drives, where hundreds of cattle were driven along this way to the market.

. They camped just outside of Sundown. While they ate their supper, Dave told Flo the story about the crooked sheriff that had tried to hang Uncle Russ for killing a crooked gambler. Only it wasn't him that did the killing, it was the mayor of the town. How his father, uncle Joe, and Aunt Anita, rode in, shot up the place, rescued Uncle Russ.

"You remember Colonel McMagee, commander of the Fort where I was a scout? Well he was a Federal Marshal at that time. He and my uncles rounded up the crooked sheriff and mayor, and their outlaw gang, put them in prison."

My father, Uncle Joe, and uncle Russ went on to serve as Cavalry Officers under the Colonel, during the great war. Laughing he said, "If you have had a belly full of Wiseman history, we better get some sleep"

The next afternoon they rode through Gila Springs. Amazed at how much it had grown. It was just a short distance out to where the Wiseman ranch was located. Dave led Flo around the valley to stop on a high knoll. He sat looking over the valley for several minutes, before he said, "Grandfather Ed, Aunt Helen, Grandfather Ben, Aunt Jenny, with Uncle Joe, and Uncle Russ, who were eighteen at the time. Sit in their covered wagon, at this spot, looking over a valley, more beautiful then, below them. Nothing but deep green grass, beautiful trees, and a crystal clear stream. "Wouldn't it be wonderful if we could sit here, side by side, each viewing their land as it were back then?"

Bob pulled Tlo to him, put his arms around her, held her tightly, and kissed her sweetly.

First, The Wind, The Snow, And The Rain

The Indians, The Explorer, The Pioneer, The Rancher

Then Alas! The Old West, Became The New West, When

The Old Ways Changed, With The Coming Of The Train

The Author